The Girl's Number Doesn't Answer

The Girl's Number Doesn't Answer

Talmage Powell

Adams Media
New York London Toronto Sydney New Delhi

Adams Media
An Imprint of Simon & Schuster, Inc.
57 Littlefield Street
Avon, Massachusetts 02322

For information about special discounts for bulk purchases, please
contact Simon & Schuster Special Sales at 1-866-506-1949 or business@
simonandschuster.com.

Manufactured in the United States of America

Library of Congress Cataloging-in-Publication Data has been applied for.

ISBN 978-1-4405-5599-2
ISBN 978-1-4405-3693-9 (ebook)

This work has been previously published in print format by:
Pocket Books of Canada, Ltd.

CAST OF CHARACTERS

THE GIRL'S
NUMBER
DOESN'T
ANSWER

CHAPTER **1** ▶▶▶ LET'S GET one thing straight at the start. He was a prince among men.

The guns are silent now. Their days of blood sacrifice are history. The world has moved on, and in great part it has forgotten.

The dead on the islands cannot remember. The living wanted to forget. The half-living will never forget. They are the gray shadows of that army that bought with its living flesh the luxury and freedom you take so much for granted.

They returned. They were carried back. Living, they are of the dead, shut away in government hospitals or in private homes. They are the shattered.

Nick Martin was one of these. He was born, he grew up, he became a Marine private after Pearl Harbor. He was a corporal when he went ashore on Iwo Jima. As a sergeant he went in with the assault waves on Okinawa.

There his luck ran out. He might have stretched it a little, but he knew what the cost would be to his company.

To him there was no decision to make. Sick as he was of the whole business, he stayed where he was. His platoon was wiped out. He held the position for another twenty minutes. It was time enough for Baker Company to get into position.

It was a little action, lost in the greater action—except to the men in Baker.

They found him with a burned-out submachine gun and grenade pins littering the ground around him. They thought at first he was dead. He had taken a machine-gun burst in the midsection as he threw the last grenade.

Nick would want you to enjoy your dinner. So I won't go into detail about what those slugs did to his guts and spine. A case-hardened medic vomited as he loaded Nick onto a stretcher.

The years have passed now, a pleasant haze of memory for most of us. We've had to look for and dream up most of our troubles. We've worked, played, groused about bills, eaten like sultans, traded our shiny cars because there was a newer model.

For Nick the years have been about eight million minutes never far from pain. His calendar has been operating-room schedules in government hospitals. His country has never ceased trying to work a miracle over him. He was patched, pieced together, carved, remade. He came to dream of gleaming scalpels, the nightmare of sleep no more horrible than that of waking reality.

He was helped. He could use his hands. Later he learned to walk. Somehow, he endured.

Maybe it was because he was never completely alone. There was always Helen, his wife, living her own eight million minutes.

I hadn't slept much since Nick and Helen Martin had disappeared day before yesterday. I wasn't feeling kindly toward the world. The end for Nick looked as if it would be the final cruelty, the ultimate irony.

It had been a scorching day, such as you find only in Tampa. I've been in Florida nearly seventeen years, and

I've never got used to the heat. If you asked me why I stay, I guess I couldn't give you a reason.

The lettering on my office door reads NATIONWIDE DETECTIVE AGENCY, SOUTHEASTERN OFFICE. AGENT IN CHARGE: ED RIVERS.

I was on the skids when I wandered into Tampa years ago. Nationwide gave me a break, a chance. So maybe there is a reason after all.

I'd looked everywhere for Nick. I don't know what I hoped to do for him. Protect him somehow. Reach him before the cops did. Stop him from doing anything more foolish. The cops wouldn't take chances, and I couldn't blame them. You don't take chances when you're looking for a man who apparently has taken a souvenir samurai sword and chopped a whole family of Japanese-Americans in little pieces.

I came back to my apartment on the edge of Tampa's Ybor City, the Latin quarter. In an old building spiced with the Spanish language and the lingering smell of Cuban sausage, the apartment is just a place to flop and eat. There is a day bed where I sleep, boiling in my own sweat, a second-hand TV I don't watch very much, a kitchenette where I can cook a little, and a bathroom with gargling plumbing and an old-fashioned tub that's big.

I ran the tub nearly to the brim with water from the cold tap, stripped off my baggy slacks and sweat-stained sport shirt. I'd left my lightweight jacket and the .38 in the bed-sitting room. I finished undressing by taking off my shoes, socks, shorts, and the knife I wear in a sheath at the nape of my neck. I've had need of the knife about once every five years. On each occasion, I'd have lost five years of living if the knife hadn't been handy.

With sweat rivuleting down the creases in my face and through the heavy brush on my chest, I grunted my nearly two-hundred-pound bulk into the tub. I didn't get a chance to soak out any of the heat. Somebody began banging on the door.

I yelled that I was coming. I dressed quickly and opened the door.

The caller was Lieutenant Steve Ivey. He was a quiet, clean-living, hard-working cop of middle age. About my size, though he didn't have the slope shoulders, and he gave the false impression of being taller.

In the department set-up, Ivey had replaced a knife blade named Julian Patrick, who'd thought more of his personal ambition than of his city. A patient city had finally got rid of Patrick. Ivey was less brilliant, but his integrity made up for it.

Ivey had never dealt directly with me before. Now he studied me for a moment; the apartment that was my background; then me, personally and coolly, his eyes starting at my shoes, moving up the bearishness of my body, coming to rest on my face. My face usually gets a reaction. I've seen it fire the eyes of women with feelings ranging from acute distaste to hot hunger. It's brought caution to some men, and a bristling, instinctive challenge to others.

Ivey was a man who was certain of himself, his strength, his capabilities. He accepted my face with a pleasant smile.

"Mind if I come in, Rivers?"

"You're welcome any time."

"Thanks." He closed the door and took off his Panama. My gray-tinged brown mat is a little thin at the crown of my head, but Ivey was bald as a fresh-peeled egg. Top his fleshiness and mild good humor with the egg, and you felt he might be found in the front row at a girlie show. The only time he ever got close to one was when he led a raid.

"Beer?" I asked.

4

"Too hot. I sweat it out."

"It helps for a minute," I said. I stepped into the kitchenette, got a beer from the refrigerator, opened the can and came back sipping at it.

Ivey sat on the arm of the worn club chair near the day bed. "Figueroa is nursing some bruised feelings, Ed."

"I'm sorry about that."

"He's about the best man I've got when I want somebody tailed." His tone was cool, but he was still smiling. "How'd you manage it? You look about as clumsy as a tired old elephant, yet Figueroa swears you were sired by an Everglades panther."

"You don't really want me to give away trade secrets, do you?"

"We won't press the point."

"That's fine."

"Did you see Nick Martin?" he asked.

"I couldn't locate him. He's so hot you're on emergency in the department. Being his friend, I knew I'd be watched. If it'll help Figueroa, tell him he's the toughest man I've ever had to shake, but it didn't do me any good. No food, no sleep—and no Nick Martin. Just blisters on my feet."

"How good a friend, Ed?"

"Very good."

"Tell me."

"Why should I?"

"I'd just like to hear it."

"Okay," I said. "Once I was a cop, up in Jersey where I was born. I liked it. I worked at it. Life looked good. I had a girl. I thought she was about everything fine and decent molded into human form. Then she ran off with a punk I was trying to nail. Their car got in the way of a fast-moving freight train.

"I tried to pickle my troubles in alcohol. One morning

5

I woke up in a back alley. I was in Tampa, Florida. The alley was about as low as I could get. I got a job on the docks. Later, Nationwide gave me a chance. After the recent look I'd had of myself, I didn't know whether I could handle it. There were times when I was afraid of myself, of the weakness I'd always despised and yet discovered inside of myself.

"Along about that time, Nick was sent to the vet's hospital across the bay. Helen came down with him and took a little cottage outside Saint Petersburg.

"I was on a job when I met them. A fellow had passed some checks. Then he'd left town. His family wanted to avoid scandal. They were making the paper good, and I was out to find him and bring him home to Papa.

"I traced him to the neighborhood where Helen was living. I was asking questions. Nick was just out of the hospital. He and Helen didn't give me any help, but it was the start of a friendship. Nick was down to about a hundred and fifteen pounds, his face all caves and bones. He was hungry for talk, for the sight of a face other than more sick faces. He and Helen needed somebody. I guess I did, too.

"In the years since then, we've seen each other off and on. Nick is pure twenty-four carat and Helen—Helen is everything to Nick, and like the person that I once read into a girl in Jersey.

"Okay, Ivey? Now you know my little confession and the way I feel about these people."

"Despite a triple murder?"

I finished the beer, set the can on the window sill, and looked at the brassy heat of the day outside. "It makes no difference in the way I feel toward Nick and Helen, Ivey. Nick in his right mind would never do such a thing."

"Right mind, wrong mind—that's not for me to say, is it?"

"No."

"Only we've got him dead to rights. And the Yamashitas were upstanding citizens, good Americans."

"I know," I said.

"Sadao Yamashita ran his import business honestly and well. His wife could have been a model for all wives, if they want to be a bit like old-fashioned homemakers. Then there was the son. Ichiro. Thirty years old. Never married. Worked in his father's business. Considerably more modern in his outlook than his parents. Something of a good-time Charlie, but never a criminal blot on his record. Three people, Rivers. Their heads bashed in, then their bodies hacked with a samurai sword. Senseless, violent, brutal. You agree?"

"How could I disagree?"

"The sword is found crudely hidden in a mangrove tangle. Identified as Nick Martin's. Only two cottages out there on Caloosa Point. The Yamashitas', and the one the Martins were occupying. Now the Martins have disappeared. Anything wrong in our addition?"

I looked at him and wished he would get the hell out of there.

"I'm sorry, Ed," he said, and he meant it. "I know what Nick Martin has been through, how long and terrible the years have been for him. I know what he and a few like him did for you and me and every living soul in this country. . . . Damn it, what the hell good are words? There are too many other undeniable words, such as Yamashita's spotless record. His business was in good order. He got along well with Victor Cameron, his partner, whose own military and civilian records are equally spotless. Ichiro's little escapades were never serious enough

7

to supply a motive. There is no motive, Ed—except in the mind of Nick Martin."

He was standing now. We both simply stood for a few long seconds.

"He drank, didn't he, Ed?" Ivey said softly. "Nick, I mean."

"You grilling me?"

"Don't get funny with me! I don't need your testimony. There are more undeniable words. We've gone over this thing with a microscope.

"Day before yesterday, Helen Martin came downtown to do some shopping. Nick was alone in the cottage, just a few hundred yards from the house where some folks with yellow skins and slant eyes lived.

"Nick ordered a fifth of whisky from the package store out there near the Point. The deliveryman said Nick looked pretty haggard.

"We've learned a lot about Nick, Ed. For one thing, we've learned that when he drank he slipped back sometimes. To Okinawa. Or Iwo. They were coming at him, hordes of little men with the yellow skins and slant eyes. It was up to him to do the job that had been thrust upon his fear-crazed young shoulders, to kill and keep killing. Is the map drawn plainly enough, Ed?"

"About the drinking," I said thickly, "there's one thing you must know. He wasn't a drunkard. Nick wasn't even a good social drinker. But hospitals and operations and drugs, years of them, take their toll. Nick had a terrible dread of drugs. He'd seen men hooked on morphine and have to go back to the hospital to fight that. He drank only when the pain got really rough. Then he drank until he was anesthetized."

"Until he was out killing Japs again," Ivey said.

"No, you've got that wrong. It didn't happen every time he drank."

8

Ivey paused at the door. "It didn't have to happen every time, did it?"

He stood a moment. "I came here wondering if Nick could really count on you, Ed. I think he can. You'll call me immediately if you locate him?"

"I'd intended to do that," I said. "I don't want him doing anything that would force a cop to shoot him."

"We'll approach him with extreme caution and readiness," Ivey admitted. "By the way, what happened on that old case? The one that caused you to meet Nick and Helen? What happened to the young guy who passed the bad paper?"

"I caught him," I said.

"I figured as much. I've got another job I can put Figueroa on. When you go looking for Nick again, there won't be a tail on you."

"Thanks," I said. "For nothing."

CHAPTER **2** ▶▶▶ I WENT DOWN to the office on Cass Street in downtown Tampa to check the mail and the telephone-answering service. There is an outer office with a cracked leather couch and a couple of matching chairs, a magazine rack, and some dusty magazines. The inner office is larger, holding my desk, filing cabinet, beat-up Underwood.

I got some routine stuff out of the way—reports on burglar-alarm systems which we install and service, a contract from a new jewelry store. From now on, the store, like thousands of others across the country, would bear a small brass plaque on the doorjamb reading PROTECTED BY NATIONWIDE DETECTIVE AGENCY.

My mind wasn't on the stuff for the mail pouch. I kept thinking of Nick. Always before, there had been a little hope dangled before him.

I sealed the printed manila envelope, stamped it, carried it into the gloomy, hot corridor, and dropped it in the mail chute.

Back in the office, I covered the Underwood, stood and wiped sweat from under my chin.

The phone rang.

I picked it up. "Nationwide. Ed Rivers speaking."

"Ed—" The voice was little more than a whisper. "Ed, this is Helen."

I eased down on the edge of the desk chair. "Where are you?"

"At a motel out Grand Central. Nick wants to see you."

"Give me the address. I'll be right out. Are you all right?"

"As all right as possible."

"And Nick?"

"The same way."

I almost moaned with relief. In the back of my mind had been a fear that I hadn't admitted. The fear that Nick might have taken the one wrong step, the one big mistake that can never be rectified.

"Ed," Helen said in that soft, strained voice. "Nick wants to give himself up. He didn't do it, Ed, but nobody in the world will believe it, except you."

"Just sit tight," I said. "I'm on my way."

She gave me the address and hung up. I hit the street, got a cab, and told the driver to hurry.

Traffic was heavy, snarled on Franklin Street. And of course the drawbridge across the Hillsborough River, which slices Tampa in half, was open for a pleasure boat. The baby yacht had a small cocktail party on the aft deck, the men natty in slacks and knitted shirts, the

10

women cool and lithe-looking in shorts. The boat purred on and the bridge closed.

The cabbie fought the traffic out the artery of Grand Central. I saw the sign and jumped from the cab almost before it had stopped rolling.

I paid the driver and hurried down the walkway that led to the cottages. The motel was an old one, built before the city had swallowed this area so thoroughly. The cottages, made of wood framing and badly needing paint, were clustered about a dusty courtyard.

I reached number seven and knocked. The door opened cautiously. Then it swung wider and I slipped inside.

The two-room cottage was close and hot, with the ancient roller blinds drawn. A single lamp with a crumpled spot in the dime-store shade was burning on a table at the end of the studio couch.

For a few seconds nobody said anything. There was Helen, closing the door and leaning against it, a kind of dumb hope in her eyes and the sooty shadows of strain on her face.

She was a good-looking woman, a rather big woman, the breed with long legs, wide shoulders. The features of her face were prominent and strong, normally vigorous. Her glossy auburn hair was touched with a silver strand here and there. She was wholesomely, healthily female, rather than merely feminine.

Nick was sitting on the couch trying to grin at me. He was a tall, rangy man, big-boned, but the sort who would never go to flesh. He had big, square hands, shoulders, face. It was a gaunt face, with lines of suffering at the base of the nostrils and about the strong, full-lipped mouth. The skin was very fair and pale, drawn on its foundation of bone. Yet the face, topped with short-cut blond hair, still held the ghost of a boyishness, like the faint memory of a boy wide-eyed with the joyous wonder

11

of living. What the boy would have done with his life under different circumstances was a question that would never be answered.

"You made good time, Ed," Nick said. "Thanks for coming."

"It won't get you into any trouble with the police, will it, Ed?" Helen asked.

"No," I said, taking the chair she offered. "It won't get me into any trouble."

Helen went over and sat down beside Nick, her hands folded tightly in her lap. If she noticed the heat in the cottage, she didn't show it. A faint shiver crossed her shoulders.

"Have the police been to see you about me?" Nick asked.

"Yes. A Lieutenant Steve Ivey."

"What kind of man is he, Ed?"

"Good man. Efficient man. No razzle-dazzle. Just a good man."

"Is he looking for anybody else? Besides me?"

"No," I said.

He studied his hands for a moment. "Once I'm in custody, then, he'll close the case?"

"I guess he'll have to."

The heat was like a silent singing in the closed cottage.

"I see," Nick said.

"There is nobody else to look for," I said. "No motive. No slightest shadow of suspicion on anybody else." After a moment, I added, "I wish there were something else I could say."

"I know." He pinched the bridge of his nose between thumb and forefinger. "Ed," he said dully, "I'm tired. I know this is no good, this hiding. They'll find us eventually. I can't undergo great activity for long periods of time. I can't run very far, Ed."

12

"Nick," Helen said, and laid her hand on his.

Nick looked at me. "I can't ask Helen to do any more."

Helen looked away from his face. They'd been married a long time. But they'd had so little of marriage. They'd got married about three months before Nick had gone overseas.

"But there is something else I can't do," Nick said, a faint tremor trying to needle into the huskiness of his voice. "I just can't walk into a cell and have the door shut behind me without the faintest hope that it will ever open again."

"What do you want me to do, Nick?"

"I want you to help me."

"You know I will."

"Yes. But right now you're wondering how, if there is any way to help. You think I did it."

"I don't think you meant to do it, Nick."

"You're wrong, Ed! I didn't do it. I liked the Yamashitas, from what little I knew about them. I'm sure they felt the same way about me—us. I used to see them around their summer place there on the Point. The little old man—so quiet and kindly. He always wore a collar and tie, even in hottest weather. The tiny lady was like something off a silk-screen painting, Ed. She was devoted to her husband and home. Sort of old-fashioned. Wouldn't wear make-up, none at all. Did all her own cooking. We used to pass the time of day, Ed. They were real folks, good folks."

"And Ichiro?"

"The son," Nick said, making a complete statement of the two words. "Instinctively, I disliked him. Legally, I guess he was clean. No arrests for reckless driving or public drunkenness, but it didn't mean he didn't do those things. Lucky, I guess. Just never got picked up. In my book he was a lecherous whoremonger. A sliminess was

13

inside of him. But that was his business, not a motive for me to kill him."

The motive was in a bottle of whisky and a deep, deep writhing thing in the darkest recesses of the subconscious. But I didn't say it.

Nick wiped his palms across his forehead. "I believed like the rest of you, at first, Ed. I thought I'd done it. Drunk. Not knowing what I was doing. Ed—I hope to heaven no other mortal ever has to feel what I was feeling as Helen and I ran away from the Point. . . .

"There they were, the little old man, and Ichiro, and the old-fashioned silk-screen lady. Ichiro was in one of the bedrooms, the old man in the living room, the lady draped across the railing of the front porch. All with their heads knocked in, their bodies hacked. The little lady's hands were hanging toward the ground and the fingers were solid red—as if in death her fingernails had been made up in a grotesque, insane way. The blood had come running down her arms and dried like that.

"She was the one Helen saw. Helen had been shopping in Tampa. She came running to the house. I was asleep on the couch in the living room. I'd—knocked myself out with alcohol. It took Helen a while to get me to understand. Had I been out of the house? Had I seen anything? You see, Helen had noticed that the samurai sword was missing. She couldn't help noticing. The sword had been taken from its wall bracket and the empty sheath lay on the floor near me.

"I guess we went a little crazy, Ed. There was no sign of anyone having been out there on that small beach that day. We knew how everything would add up to look. We panicked. Ran. Came here."

Nick stopped talking. Helen sat squeezing herself very tight inside.

"Like rats in a dead-end hole," Nick said at last. "We

14

couldn't plan. We couldn't think. We grabbed some clothes from the cottage and enough money to keep us going for a few days.

"Helen could slip out after dark to buy us food, but I knew I was licked, even if I wouldn't admit it to myself right away. I started working up the courage to turn myself in. Then, today, I knew there was one hope, Ed. You."

I sat and waited, while the heavy sweat ran down the sides of my face.

"You don't have many friends, Ed," Nick said.

"I guess I don't."

"Because the word means something to you. You give a part of a kind of holy thing inside of you when you call somebody a friend. There aren't many who know it, who would suspect, looking at you. But I know it, Ed, and for the first time in my life I'm going to trade on friendship." He looked at me levelly, and said quietly, "Ed, I want you to get me out of this."

"How?"

"That's your job."

"You give me anything in the way of evidence," I said, "you give me one single grain of salt in your favor and I'll give you everything I've got."

"Maybe a grain of sand will do just as well," Nick said. He looked at Helen and nodded. She got up, crossed the room, opened the small closet. She came back to us carrying a pair of house slippers that wore a look of newness. She handed the slippers to Nick.

"This wouldn't stand for a minute in court," Nick said. "It wouldn't reopen a case when the only possible suspect is in custody. There is only my word on one point, Ed. It wouldn't mean much, under the circumstances, to a single person on this earth, except you."

He turned the slippers in his hand. "I've been nagged

15

by the feeling that there was a way of knowing for sure whether or not I went to the Yamashita cottage and killed them. Can a man do such a thing and not remember? There was something I was overlooking, something that would tell me. I couldn't pin it down. Until today, when I was putting these slippers on.

"They're a present from Helen, Ed. She gave them to me just last week. I was wearing them the afternoon the Yamashitas were killed, wearing them for the first time.

"I accepted delivery of the whisky wearing them. I went to sleep and woke up wearing them. Helen took them off me when she came home and helped me under a cold shower. In short, I was wearing these slippers during the whole time of the massacre, Ed. Here. Take them. Turn them over. Look at the soles."

I did as he asked. The soles were of soft, pliant leather, like suède.

I felt a cold, brittle thing form inside of me. A taste came to my mouth as if my teeth had a metallic edge.

I looked into Nick Martin's eyes and I would have bet my blood to the final drop that he was telling the truth about the slippers.

Then I looked again at the soles of the slippers. If he had walked the distance from his cottage to the Yamashita summerhouse and back again, the soft leather would have been full of ground-in sand.

The soles of the slippers were as clean as Nick Martin's courage.

CHAPTER **3** ▶▶▶ IN A PHONE BOOTH at the corner drugstore, I had all the numbers dialed except the last one. I hesitated before I gave the dial that final spin.

The question pulsed in my mind and brought a small feeling of suffocation to the phone booth: Presuming Nick's innocence, could I do anything about it? A stranger's life and trust would have been inviolable—and this was Nick. Did I have the right to dial the final number and wait for a phone to ring downtown? Once the steel closed around Nick, everything would depend on me.

I had no starting point, nothing. The slippers were negative evidence. I was the only one who would accept and believe their meaning. At that, they simply indicated that he'd been asleep while an inhuman fiend had slaughtered three people and framed an innocent man without compunction.

I had to start out by believing in the existence of this fiend with no evidence of it.

I hadn't even the clue to a character pattern to help. His was not merely a criminal mind. He might never have killed before. He might never kill again. He could be a wanderer, a thousand miles away by now. His might be a bland, everyday face on a Tampa street at this moment.

There was an alternative, which I hadn't mentioned to Nick or Helen. I had connections in Ybor City, some extending to a political refugee or two from a revolution in a Latin country. In swarming Ybor City, the grave gentleman playing dominoes in one of the old men's clubs might yesterday have been a secretary of state. I knew one man who might help get Nick out of the country. Central and South American revolutions had been hatched over rum toddies in Ybor City. A matter this small could be handled.

With Nick out of the way, the pressure on me would not be so great.

And that gave me the insight to my thinking.

I was thinking of myself, not of Nick or Helen. Flight on Nick's part would entail hardship and privation. It could cost him his life.

I can't run very far, Ed.

An old war, like a story of not-quite-real goblins to today's kids, had taken care of that.

I spun the dial.

After a moment, I got Ivey.

"I have Nick Martin," I said.

"Where are you?"

"We'll get to that. There's a condition."

"I can't bargain, Rivers."

"Want me to hang up?"

"What is it?"

"I know Nick will be treated as decently as possible," I said. "You're doing a job that you have to do; you're not out for blood."

"That's right."

"I want you to understand one thing clearly. I didn't find Nick. He called me. The surrender is his own doing and entirely voluntary on his part."

"What's your condition?"

"Patience, Ivey. One more thing I want you to know. I believe that Nick is innocent. I wish you would too, but I'm not counting on your being able to do anything about it. You've got too many official strings on you. I haven't, and I'm going to act on the belief."

Ivey said nothing.

"Now we get to the condition," I said. "Technically, Helen Martin aided and abetted her husband's flight. Turn your back on all human elements, and you could call her an accessory after the fact. It's a technicality I can't stomach, circumstances being what they are. I don't think Nick could, either. I don't think he's thought of it yet. He's been too busy thinking about the way he fancies he's dragged her into hiding."

"You're pretty free with suggestions, Rivers. I expect to hear another any second."

"And it's a simple one, Ivey. Write into the record that she was forced into it, that she did it under duress."

"Let her go free?"

"She won't be free," I said, "as long as Nick is in a cell. You won't have to warn her or have any men watching her to keep her from leaving Tampa."

Ivey thought about it briefly. "I can't prove she left the cottage on the Point with him, unless one of them admitted it. If he happened to be alone when I picked him up, I wouldn't have much of a case on her."

"All right," I said. Then I told him where Nick was.

Ivey's knock sounded on the motel shanty door about twenty minutes later. Nick and I were alone in the place. I crossed the front room and opened the door.

Ivey came in, looked at me, then at Nick. He took off his Panama, wiped the sweatband with his fingers.

"Nick Martin?" Ivey asked.

"Yes," Nick said.

"Are you ready?"

19

"Yes."

Nick rose slowly from the couch, picked up a small suitcase. Now that the moment was here, I could see the sinking sickness hit him inside. It showed in his eyes. He tried to grin it out. "Okay if I take my toothbrush?"

"Sure," Ivey said.

Nick moved to the door, his tall, spare body hunched. "Well, Ed—" He stood trying to keep the grin on his gaunt face, wiping the palm of his free hand on the thigh of his pants. He raised the hand, balled it into a fist, and chunked me on the shoulder. "Don't forget how to duck, old son."

"Don't worry," I said. "I'll be seeing you."

Nick looked at Ivey. "What are we waiting for?" He stepped into the courtyard and started toward the street.

I watched a uniformed cop get out of a patrol car parked at the curb. He opened the door of the car and Nick and Ivey got in.

The car pulled away, with Nick looking straight ahead.

I closed the cottage and went down the street to the restaurant where Helen was waiting. The place was narrow and gloomy. She sat in one of the crude wooden booths near the front.

I squeezed across the booth from her.

She sat twisting a paper napkin in her fingers. She looked at me with a dazed sorrow dulling her eyes. She didn't need to ask questions, and she was determined not to make a display.

"It's almost dinnertime," I said. "We'll go downtown to eat."

"I'd rather find a place to stay first, Ed."

"Okay."

"Would you mind—getting my things from the motel? They're all packed. I'd rather not go back."

"It'll only take a minute," I said.

20

I walked to the motel, picked up the two suitcases by the cottage door. I left the tagged key in the lock when I closed the cottage door from outside.

A young, squat, dark man in a rumpled sport shirt and slacks stepped from the manager's cottage as I carried the bags toward the street.

"I saw the cop car," he said. "What's with the couple in number seven?"

"They won't be back. The lady asked me to get her bags."

"I dunno . . ."

"The lady is in the greasy spoon down the street if you want her O.K."

"I guess I better."

"They owe you anything?"

"Nah, but I don't want any beefs about lost luggage."

He shuffled along beside me toward the restaurant. "What's with them, anyway? Why the cops?"

"They took a wooden nickel."

"Smart guy, huh?"

"Just not talkative," I said.

He followed me into the restaurant. Helen rose as I went toward her. The manager craned his neck to look her up and down.

"She's accepted the luggage," I said, putting the bags down and tapping him on the shoulder. "Now scram."

He looked at my face and backed off, with a sneer of bravado forming on his lips. He walked out of the place with a tough, swaggering gait.

The Martin car took us apartment-hunting.

We found her a place on Florida Avenue. Downtown, the street is a main drag in the business district. As it pushes out mile by mile, stores, shops, and office buildings give way to garages, used-car lots, and one-time grand old

21

gingerbread homes which have been converted to apartment buildings and rooming houses.

An ad in the classified section of the newspaper led us to a rambling, three-story white house. The apartment was small, but clean and comfortable—not bad for what Helen could afford to pay. It consisted of a tiny sitting room, a bedroom with a bay window overlooking the hustle and noise of the street, and a small kitchen with apartment-size refrigerator and gas stove. A pay phone was right outside the door in the hallway. I took note of the number.

When the placid, bovine landlady had completed her quiz, accepted Helen's money, and plodded downstairs, I carried Helen's bags into the bedroom.

"Sure you won't eat downtown?" I asked.

"No, I'll fix something here."

"I'll be in touch."

"Thanks for everything, Ed."

She was standing with her back to me, looking out the window.

I left quickly.

When a woman has reached the point where she must weep alone, she's entitled to that much privacy.

I had a Cuban sandwich and a pint of cold beer for dinner.

Twilight came like a hot mist rising from the river. People dallied in cocktail lounges and restaurants. A fresh edition of one of the papers hit the street with Nick Martin's picture on the front page.

I wondered if the fiend was still in Tampa to enjoy the photography—somewhere in a plush apartment, or a pink-and-proper stucco in a subdivision, or a vermin-ridden hole in West Tampa or Ybor City.

Relax, fiend. Take your first deep breath in two days.

22

It was the only hope I had at the moment. I wouldn't think of the alternative—that he was eating in Atlanta, or hitching a ride in the Carolinas, or stoking the boilers in a freighter that had pulled out of Port Tampa for South America.

I made my way through the theater and window-shopping crowds on Franklin Street, went up to the office on Cass, and turned a light on.

I work for a big outfit, and there's a routine I have to follow.

I took out the triplicate forms and filled them out. Employer's name: Helen Martin. Nature of investigation: Husband arrested on suspicion of murder.

After I'd scrawled a signature that could be mistaken for Helen Martin's, I took out my checkbook and eyed the balance. I work on a salary-commission setup. There was enough in the bank to pay a retainer for several days. Meantime, my salary-commission checks would be coming through. I could keep the financial cycle in motion for a considerable time until the home office cuts dried it up.

With the report ready for the mail, I went around the corner to the *Journal* building. Ed Price was on the city desk. We swapped our usual and obvious "Hello, Ed."

"I want to see some files in your morgue," I said.

"Library's closed. Librarian goes home at five o'clock, Ed. You know that." A tall, lean man, Price dropped a copy pencil on his desk, stood up.

I followed him out of the office, down the corridor. "What's the story," he asked.

"None yet."

"The Yamashita thing?"

"You're a close guesser."

"Yeah, I'm a walking ouija board. You're Nick Martin's close friend. Today he surrenders. Somebody arranged that." Price stopped before a heavy wooden door.

"I'm doing this for nothing," he said.

"The *Journal's* been my favorite paper in the past."

"I know. Hence, the favor. You haven't a chance in hell of helping Nick Martin. Under the setup you couldn't even frame somebody else for the job."

Price unlocked the door and clicked a switch, and long fluorescent lights went on overhead. The newspaper morgue smelled warmly and mustily of newsprint and paste.

Price rolled open drawers and carried a small stack of clippings in manila envelopes and photographs to a table. I sat down and he parked his skinny rump against the edge of a nearby table.

He lighted a cigarette, folded his thin, pale arms, and stood chewing the end of the fag as he smoked.

"This should be good," he said. "This appeals to the perverted sense of humor you seem to pick up around a newspaper office. Wish I could go every step with you, Ed, until you bust a gut with frustration. Man ought to learn something about the meaning of life, watching a bull beat his brains out charging a wall of nothingness."

CHAPTER **4** ▶ ▶ ▶ THE FILE on the murder had started lustily and grown fatter as each edition came off the presses. I waded through the gory pictures and details. Most of it I knew. Like all authentic horror, the story was too simple and stark to need much embellishment for effect.

Photographic coverage had been extensive. Price had an innate sense of taste under his cynicism which had kept him from running some of the worst of the pictures.

From a particularly gruesome group, I got one fresh detail. At the time of death, Ichiro, the thirty-year-old son, had been wearing Bermuda shorts, sport shirt, and barefoot sandals. Both parents had been fully clothed in street wear. The garb of the parents jibed with a small detail in one of the stories, to the effect that Mr. and Mrs. Yamashita had had a restaurant reservation for dinner that night but had canceled it.

I added one more small detail. Ichiro had a private apartment in town. My mental camera dollied to give me a glimpse of the afternoon of violence from a new angle. Ichiro choosing the cottage for some purpose of his own, believing he would have privacy until after dinnertime. The parents changing their minds, returning to the cottage, and being murdered for the very simple reason that they showed up at an inopportune moment.

I passed on to the Victor Cameron file. It was thin. There was a shot of him as reporters had broken the news to him the day of his partner's death.

The photo showed Cameron as a big, gray, tired-looking man. There was some semblance of military bearing and discipline in his shoulders and face, but it was a quality that had almost faded from existence.

I compared the recent shot with one taken over ten years ago when he'd come to Tampa and the import enterprise had been written up in the Sunday business section.

He had changed considerably. Ten years ago even a camera could catch his air of command. He'd looked brisk, efficient, intolerant, and superior. I wondered if in the intolerance and superiority there had been the seeds of inner anxiety and uncertainty, that had grown to bring the change in him.

The spread gave some accounting of his background. He came from an old and well-known New England family. A colonel, he had filled a desk post in Washington during the war. Sent to Japan during the Occupation, he had left his wife and small daughter in the United States. He had returned to the States after the accidental death of his wife. He had brought his daughter to Florida to live, eventually entering the import business with Yamashita.

I assumed that Cameron was valuable to Yamashita as a partner, being an American who also possessed the fine qualification of having good connections in Japan.

Two points itched me. Why Cameron had stayed such a long time in the Orient without his family, and the kind of accident that had killed his wife. The explanations were probably perfectly innocent, but anything that veers from the norm bothers me.

I drove a rented car out to the Cameron address. It was on Davis Islands, the plush development pumped from the bottom of the bay during the boom of the 1920's.

Across the bridge linking Davis Islands to the mainland boulevard, I cruised down a wide, beautiful street lined with tall royal palms. Behind the neat lawns, the houses were big, Spanish, heavy with wealth.

I came abreast of a pair of white stone pillars hugging a driveway and linked overhead by filigreed ironwork. The number 76 was on one of the pillars, in black block form. I turned into the drive.

A screen of flowering shrubs and Australian pines hid the house until I rounded a bend in the driveway.

I parked the rented heap and got out.

A single light glowed softly in the fore part of the house. I mounted the pillared veranda and pressed the door buzzer.

I tried a second and third time. No one answered. I walked to the edge of the veranda. The moonlit night was quiet. From somewhere back of the house came the sudden sound of a loud splash.

I dropped from the veranda and walked around the side

of the house. The short-clipped grass was so luxuriant it was like tiny springs under my feet, a rich green carpet for the shrubs and trimmed hedges of the landscaping.

Rounding the rear corner of the house, I saw moonlight glinting on water. The pool was large enough to have done credit to a small-town country club. It was in pale tile, with a diving board and tower at my end.

The wake of ripples reached the far end of the pool, reversed direction and came back. The strokes of the swimmer were slow, easy, graceful. She came out of the water dripping and gleaming in the moonlight. She stood on the edge of the pool, small, perfectly made, vibrant as a kitten. She took off her bathing cap, taloned her fingers, and scratched her boyish-cut black hair into a careless jumble.

She saw me when she started from the pool's edge toward the house. She stopped, her manner showing no fright.

"I beg your pardon," I said. "I was looking for Mr. Cameron. I heard your last dive and came around to see if maybe it was him."

"You might try the doorbell," she said. She had a lazy, soft voice with boredom and insolence resting in its depths.

"I did. Three times."

She walked toward me with her careless, abandoned stride. She stopped about four feet away, tilted her head, and studied me. "I'm Rachie Cameron," she said. "Who are you, ugly man?"

"The name is Ed Rivers," I said. "When will Mr. Cameron be home?"

"He's inside now. He said he was going to shower and retire early. You just didn't give him time to get to the door, that's all."

She let her hips swing as she walked ahead of me toward the house. Her one-piece white bathing suit was adequate,

27

even prim, but she managed to transform its lines to something less than bikini.

We crossed a flagstone patio decorated with beach chairs, outdoor grill, white, wrought-iron table and chairs.

She opened twin glass doors, turned on a soft overhead light. We were in a long playroom. She went to the bar at the farther end.

"Drink?"

"A beer if you have it."

She laughed. "Beer, of course. I should have known, looking at you. I'll have the same."

She went behind the bar, came across the room with two beers in tall, cone-shaped glasses.

She offered one of the glasses. She didn't let it go right away, and we both stood holding it for a second.

"What kind of business are you in, ugly man?"

"I'm a private detective."

"Really?" She seemed interested, but not in my occupation.

She stepped back. The bored, vacant look was gone from her dark eyes for a moment. "Good old plebeian beer," she said. "Here's to big, ugly men who drink beer."

She took a long pull at the beer, set the glass on a table, and reached for a beach robe lying on a rattan chair. She slipped the robe over her shoulders and put her feet in Oriental sandals that were on the floor near the chair.

She sat down with her legs stretched before her. They were slim, lithe, deeply tanned.

"My father hire you?"

"No."

"Of course you'd say that."

"Any reason why he should?"

"Me," she said.

"Really?"

"I'm a bad one." She grinned. "Sure he didn't retain you to keep me out of trouble?"

"Positive. Have you ever been in trouble before?"

"No. I'm careful."

"I guess that pays."

She motioned toward a chair. "Why don't you sit down? I won't bite."

"I came to see your father," I reminded her.

"He's probably knocked himself out with a double dose of Seconal. Do you take sleeping pills?"

"I'm afraid it's a modern habit I've not adopted."

"Shake, pal. It means you don't give a damn."

"That one curved right out of my mitt," I said.

She shrugged. "It's just people who give a damn who can't sleep."

"Rachie," I said, "you've been reading too many books. You've got a corkscrew in your thinking."

"Really?" she smiled. "I'd like to hear your views sometime."

"I'm afraid they'd be a little old-fashioned for you."

"How nice!" she said with animation. "A virtuous American! A big, ugly, virtuous American male! I'll bet you stand at attention when the flag goes by."

"I manage to get my hat off," I said. "If you'll tell your father I want to get in touch with him . . ."

"Why?" Cameron demanded.

I turned, and he was standing in the doorway behind me. The bigness of him was clothed in the finest slacks and sport shirt. The shirt was open at the throat. His iron-gray hair was still damp from his shower. He tried to look solidly commanding. He couldn't quite pull the tired edges together.

I introduced myself, pulled out my wallet, and showed him the photostat of my license, as his strap sandals padded into the playroom.

29

"I can't imagine what business you have here, Mr. Rivers."

"I'm working on the Yamashita case."

"Oh? In what capacity?"

"I've been retained by the man the police have in custody."

"I should think you'd be ashamed to take his money," he said, "but I suppose to a man like you a job is a job."

"You can suppose anything you like. It's your privilege."

"If you feel you have to go through the motions," he said, "you may report to your employer that you made a call here. Good night, Mr. Rivers."

"I think you'd better get one thing straight. I never make motions for their own sake."

"I see." A glint of caution came to his gray eyes. He turned brusquely and made deliberate movements to the bar. He poured himself a stiff hooker of whisky.

Rachie stretched and said, "Pour a drink for me, Papa." She broke the final word in two, pronouncing it as I understand the French do.

"You drink too much," he told her. "I want you to go to your room."

"I prefer not to," she said with a hateful simplicity.

As they faced each other, the room was tainted with a sense of old battles, many battles. Their wills wrestled for a moment. Then Cameron tossed off his drink angrily.

"Well," he shouted at me, "don't stand there like the caricature of a phlegmatic Buddha! The door's open and waiting for you."

"Thanks," I said. "But I came hoping to learn something about the Yamashitas, not witness a man's defeat by an incorrigible daughter."

"Bravo, ugly man!" Rachie said with a little pip of delighted laughter.

30

Cameron turned deep red. Clear across the room I could hear him pulling in his breath.

"Whoever you are, Rivers, I don't like you."

"I'm sorry."

"My first disappointment in you," Rachie said. "An apology from the ugly man. You're trying to butter him up."

"Keep out of this," Cameron said to her.

"Papa, I shall say whatever I damn well—"

"You heard him," I said.

Her eyes caught mine. I felt my nostrils flare. She didn't curl herself in the chair, but she gave that impression. "Yes, sir," she said.

I turned my attention to Victor Cameron. "You certainly can't mind a few questions about the Yamashitas."

"I can, and do."

"I don't mind," Rachie said.

The old lion's tail had been twisted until the spirit had been milked out of him. As Cameron looked at his daughter, at the twisted excitement and pleasure in her, I could feel the gray shadows closing over his spirit.

CHAPTER **5** ▶ ▶ ▶ CAMERON MADE a motion with his hand. I followed him out of the playroom.

We moved down a hallway for a short distance and turned into a study furnished with leather and walnut.

He closed the door, crossed to the walnut desk, and sat down in a leather chair.

"I can't see what you possibly hope to gain by this, Rivers."

"Information."

"The police have information. I suggest you see them."

"I have. I've read the papers, too."

"Then why me?"

"Because you knew them, the Yamashitas, better than anyone else."

"I've told the police everything I know."

"You've answered their questions," I agreed. "Questions based on the belief that Nick Martin is the guilty man. I don't share the belief. Somewhere there is a man or woman who murdered three people and left an innocent man to pay for the crime. I don't want to go after a person so violent and desperate. I'm afraid of such a person. I didn't ask for the job, any more than Nick Martin chose his role. The job caved in on me and trapped me in the bloody debris. So you see, Cameron, this unknown person and I are linked by the common bond of desperation and fear. There's just one way for me to cut the link. And when I find him or her, I'll know the kind of person I'm dealing with."

Light from the desk lamp caught in his eyes. It hardened their grayness and deepened the already deep sockets. "You're crazy, you know."

"If you mean I don't share some of your values, you're right."

"What is Nick Martin to you?"

"He's my friend."

"And what is a friend? They come into your house, they drink your liquor, they go away again. Shadows."

"I won't argue. I just want information."

"You spoke of there being only one way out for you," he said. "There is another. Surely you've thought of it. I don't

32

know why you believe in Martin's innocence. I don't care. I know that a sensible man would see his proper course of conduct and leave police matters to the police."

"That would be a very agreeable line of thought," I said, "if I could string it through my head."

"You'd forget Nick Martin. You'd know you were not to blame."

"That's a respectable way of looking at it," I said.

"Of course it is. I know what I'm talking about."

"Are you buying, Cameron?"

"You must have a price. Nick Martin bought," Cameron said. "He couldn't have paid much, a broken-down war vet living on pension checks."

I put my knuckles on the edge of his desk and forced them to stay there. I leaned toward him and smiled. "Why do you want to buy me, Cameron?"

His eyes lost some of their age. "I don't," he said. "It was your suggestion."

"You would have paid."

"The guilty man is in jail," he said. "I don't know what your game is, but it's obvious you're up to something devious and dirty in the hopes of making some money. Certainly I'd have paid—and then promptly had you jailed for extortion."

He got up, came around the desk, crossed the thick carpeting of the study, and opened the door.

"Good night, Rivers."

I leaned against the edge of the desk. A drop of sweat seeped into the corner of my mouth.

"Did you go out to the Yamashita summerhouse the day of the killings?"

He stood silent for a moment deciding whether or not he would answer. "No," he said. He added, "I can't prove it. I didn't know I'd ever need to prove it. The police find my word sufficient. I trust you will, also."

33

"Did the senior Yamashita have a business appointment that afternoon?"

"He might have had a personal appointment, but it's highly unlikely. He didn't mix business and his home life."

"Do you know why he and his wife canceled their restaurant reservation that day?"

"I suppose," he said, acid eating deeper into his voice, "that it was because they changed their minds and decided to dine at home. People do such things very innocently on occasion, you know."

"Who did Ichiro meet out there that afternoon?"

"I knew very little of Ichiro's personal affairs. I haven't heard that he met someone. How did you dream the question up, Rivers?"

"It just seeped in my mind out of the heat," I said. "Someone was out there."

"Of course. A real bad man who nobody saw went all the way out to Caloosa Point because there was a handy veteran who could be framed, killed three people for no reason whatever, framed said veteran, and vanished. I'm afraid it's a delusion you'll have to work out for yourself, Rivers. Now, do I have to call a police escort for you?"

"I won't put you to the bother," I said. "By the way, will you keep the business going?"

His knuckles showed white where he gripped the edge of the door. "I believe that's my affair. You've goaded me far enough, Rivers. The truth is blunt and simple. Sadao was a refined, good, and successful man. He lived a simple, honest life. Our business prospered and was in excellent condition. I could talk to you a million years and not add anything more. But I don't intend talking to you any longer."

As I passed through the door, he said, "Don't come back, Rivers."

"Thanks," I said. "It's been an interesting evening."

He followed me down the hallway and slammed the front door behind me.

I stood on the veranda for a moment catching the faint breeze that came off the bay. Then I got in the rented heap and drove it to the rental garage. I rode a city bus to Ybor City.

It had been a long day and the shadows were long over the narrow streets and rusty, iron-filigree balconies on the old buildings. Traffic was moderately heavy but seemed to move in a silent rush. Muffled Latin rhythm pulsed like a sensual, tropical heartbeat from behind the shutters of a private club. From one of the ancient brick buildings crowding and frowning over the sidewalk a girl came forth. She had a great mane of coal-black frizzled hair with a flower in it. She wore a red dress that sheened in the street-lamp glow like satin, and spike-heel shoes. Her body was lush, almost heavy. As I passed the light, she glanced at me. For only a moment. She was after slicker, better-heeled prey. Her face was childish, with skin like the light-tan, silken leaf Ybor City cigar-makers use for the outer wrappers on the expensive smokes. Her eyes were jet black, heavy with mascara and weariness. She was all of fifteen or sixteen. At twenty, she'd be a hag.

From Davis Islands to Ybor City wasn't such a jump, after all. The nameless girl and Rachie Cameron had a lot in common. Both were lost. Their differences were minor. Rachie was considerably older. And Rachie had much more money.

I turned in at the all-night market on the corner, bought my usual twenty-five-pound block of ice, and carried it up to the apartment.

I put the ice in a pan, the pan on the table, and an electric fan behind the pan. I pointed the fan at the day bed, blowing over the ice.

Then I stripped to my shorts and turned in.

35

Strain was not so deeply etched on Helen Martin's strongly beautiful face the next morning. She wore a crisp cotton dress and had her silver-threaded auburn hair pulled back and bunned neatly. She was still in there pitching.

She closed her apartment door after I entered and asked if I'd care for something cool to drink. I'd breakfasted on soft-fried eggs chased by a pint of icy beer.

"I have some orange juice," Helen suggested.

I nodded and she stepped into the kitchenette to get it.

"Ed," she said, as I accepted the glass, "I'm terribly ashamed of us. Neither Nick nor I thought of it yesterday."

"Thought of what?"

"Your retainer."

"My feelings are delicate," I said. "Don't stick pins in them."

"Nick had a trusty call me this morning, to make sure I was all right—and to tell you we have a little money in savings."

"I'm on vacation," I said, "and taking a busman's holiday."

She looked at me gravely. "All right, Ed," she said with the kind of self-respecting simplicity that I like, "and thank you very much."

"Now that we're over that hurdle, what are you doing for a while?"

"Anything I can to help Nick."

"I'm going to case an apartment. I want you to go along. You might see and make sense of something I'd overlook."

"Must be the residence of someone I know."

"Ichiro Yamashita's."

"I didn't know him very well, Ed. Even less than his parents. Have you found out something?"

"I'm still groping," I said, "but I'm beginning to see the first edges of a pattern."

Ichiro had lived on the top floor of a five-story apart-

36

ment building on Bayshore Boulevard. The building was modern, with small balconies and terraces landscaped with baby potted palms for each level. At ground level there was a courtyard with a small pool. The pool was bedecked with lily pads and fed from a sparkling fountain.

Helen and I stepped from the self-service elevator on Ichiro's floor. The air-conditioning brought a grateful response from my skin. The corridor was perfectly silent. I suspected the builder hadn't neglected soundproofing.

We passed a pair of potted palms nestling on either side of a large hall mirror, and stopped before the smooth blond surface of a door.

I had the door open in something like three minutes, using the hair-thin sliver of steel on my key ring.

The apartment coaxed the senses. We stood on a small landing from which a short tier of stairs, railed with wrought iron, led to the spacious living room. The modern furnishings were set about with an air of carelessness. On one wall was hung a large painting, very eye catching, of a nude. The inner wall was paneled with wormy cypress, the outer was a bank of glass with sliding glass panels opening onto the terrace. The terrace gave a startling view of the divided boulevard below and the stretches of the sun-dappled bay beyond.

Near the entrance to the kitchen there was a small bar of wormy cypress. Back of the bar the glasses were neatly stacked. I went behind the bar and looked at the labels on the stock. Ichiro had had expensive tastes in liquor.

As I turned, I glanced beneath the bar. I picked up a bottle with a strange black label, opened it, smelled the contents, and amended my impression. He'd also had most erotic tastes.

"What is it?" Helen asked.

"Absinthe." A liqueur made of wormwood and brandy. Outlawed stuff. It does strange things to the senses. If

37

imbibed freely enough it eventually eats holes in the brain.

A circuit of the apartment revealed only further details of the den of a sensualist. Labels on the albums for the hi-fi outfit indicated Ichiro's addiction to the erotic offshoots of the school of progressive jazz. Books were not in abundance; a small case held several copies of privately printed editions.

As Helen and I completed our tour in the small, gleaming kitchen, I heard a scratching on the living-room door.

I pushed her behind me and stood with the open kitchen door concealing us.

The lock was keyed open. The door swung back. A man entered the apartment.

He closed the door quickly and stood a moment on the landing.

He could have hired out to frighten little children—a hairless gorilla in imitation Brooks Brothers. His face was flat, swarthy, Oriental in cast—not the Orient of paper umbrellas or dainty painting on translucent china; the Orient that had spawned the hordes of Genghis Khan.

With his massive shoulders and short legs he looked top heavy. But he had the grace of a dancer as he stepped into the living room.

He stood for a second pause, his pear-shaped head with its sparse growth of coarse black hair tilted to one side.

Wheeling, he passed out of my range of vision. I heard him rummaging in the bedroom, opening drawers.

I felt that I should know him, but I couldn't place him.

His search of the bedroom took two or three minutes. I eased out of the kitchen. The carpet deadened my footfalls as I slid to the bedroom door.

CHAPTER **6** ►►► WHEN HE came out of the bedroom, I threw my right arm around his chin from behind. His neck was so short I couldn't clamp the grip on his throat, but I snapped his head back, my knee in the small of his back.

His body went rigid for a second.

"Who are you?" I said. "What are you looking for here?"

There was fine sweat on the roll of thick, swarthy flesh at the base of his head, a moisture mingled with the roots of the black strands scattered on top of the pear.

He was held powerless. He seemed immobile from fright. I equaled him in weight, topped him three inches in height, had every advantage.

Then something happened.

My body was snapped so hard it felt as if all its vertebrae were hot slugs of metal crunching together. The room upended. I crashed into a cocktail table with my shoulder.

Before I could reassemble the smashed pieces of what had been me, he said, "Hah!" very gutturally in his throat. He leaped at me like a bowlegged chimpanzee.

His legs extended before him, he came down with his rump stopped by my rib cage. I heard grindings inside of

39

myself and felt as if splinters had been jabbed into every nerve.

He bounced off me. I floundered a blow at him. He brushed it aside.

"Hah!"

He grabbed my collar, jerked me half upright. I felt the corded steel of his arms encircle my neck.

I tried to kick him, slug him, bite him. I wasn't proud. I'd have fought in any manner to get out of that grip.

He turned on the pressure, his knees half bent, his body rocked back. It felt as if my head were being torn off by the roots.

"Hah!"

He shifted his hold faster than a flea can jump. I sensed the swivel of his hips, the snap of his body. I was weightless for a second. Then I hit a chair and carried it into the wall with me.

I was in a small boat on a very rough sea and I was seasick as hell. Somewhere off in the gray mists three indistinct pear-shaped heads floated. All were contorted with a savage, battle-hungry pleasure.

All three hazy faces swooped toward me.

Then they disappeared. I heard the dull, heavy sound of his body falling to the carpet.

I managed to turn my eyes, and there were three Helen Martins shimmering in the gray. The three had a modernistic metal statuette of a nude in their right hand. The nude had previously been on a table.

They dropped the chunk of metal and helped me to my feet. I stood with the wall supporting me and my eyes stopped playing tricks. The three Helens ran together and became one.

My gaze groped for the big bruiser. He was lying not five feet away. He'd remain there for several minutes. A lump was swelling on the crown of his head.

I fell into a chair. I thought for a moment I was going to be sick. I managed to hold onto the chair. Helen had gone somewhere. She reappeared holding a glass.

"Drink this, Ed."

I took the glass, gulped, and let the heat flood down my throat, spread through my stomach.

I felt life begin to quiver tentatively inside of me once more.

"You'd better tap that brandy bottle yourself," I said, handing Helen the glass.

"Are you all right now?"

"I'll be sore in various spots for a week," I said, "but I don't think he broke as many parts as it felt."

Helen took my advice, going to the bar and taking a jigger of brandy.

I was content for the moment to sprawl in the chair and pull air in as the ruptured feeling passed from my lungs.

"I've taken beatings," I told Helen, "but never before from a man my own size who started at such a disadvantage. I must be slipping or getting old."

"You should watch television more. Sure you're all right?"

"I'm coming around. Why watch television?"

"You might have recognized him if you'd ever caught any of the big-time wrestling programs. He's Prince Kuriacha. He was heavyweight wrestling champion of the world for a while."

"They shouldn't let him out without handcuffs and muzzle."

Prince Kuriacha groaned. He rolled to his side, lifted his hand, touched the lump on his head. He groaned a second time, put his palms on the carpet, and pushed himself to a half-sitting position.

As he opened his eyes and raised his head, he found himself staring into the small end of the .38.

41

He was temporarily immobile, his eyes drops of black ink in yellow tallow.

"You can have that chair," I said. "But don't make any sudden motions."

He went sliding across the carpet on his behind and pulled himself into the silken-covered club chair.

He took a linen handkerchief from the breast pocket of his natty tropical suit. He gingerly made a compress, holding the handkerchief on his pump knot. He squinted at Helen. "A doll," he said. "Flattened by a doll. How do you like that!"

He added in my direction, "I'd have turned you inside out, you know." He spoke without particular rancor or fear. No trace of accent was in his voice. It wasn't a beautiful voice. It had a sound like dry cereal being walked on by someone in heavy boots.

"You a cop?" he asked.

"In a way." Given the chance to look him over in detail, I decided the Prince must be very well heeled from his years of big-time wrestling showmanship. Suits like that pale-gray tropical didn't come cheap. His shoes looked like hand-sewn Italian loafers. The diamond on his little finger was like the beacon stolen from a lighthouse. The watch on the big, oaken wrist was made of platinum and diamonds.

"What kind of answer is that?" he said. "You're either a cop or not a cop."

"I'm cop enough for the moment. Cop enough to ask some questions," I said.

"Such as?"

"What brought you here?"

"A camera."

"You'd better explain."

"It's simple. Ichiro Yamashita borrowed a camera from me, a really good camera. Kind of a keepsake. A movie star gave it to me when I was appearing on the coast, just before she married her fourth husband. What with the court tying up the estate and all, I figured the only way I'd ever get the camera back was to sneak up here and take it."

"A direct, blunt course of action."

"Well," he said, "I've been accused of being that kind of man. Now it's my turn. Who the hell are you?"

I told him, adding an explanation about Helen.

He sat thinking about it. "You're guilty of breaking and entering, you know."

"So are you."

"Yeah. That leaves us kind of even, don't it?"

"Not exactly," I pointed out. "I have a private operator's license, and in this case I'm working under a certain amount of police sanction."

"I tell you what," he said affably. "Let's just call it even and forget the whole thing."

"I've got another question or two."

"Maybe I'm tired of talking."

I glanced at Helen. "Call the police."

"Now wait a minute!" Kuriacha said. "I'm a respectable man. I've got my reputation to think about. Newspaper reporters are always after a guy in my position. They say it makes for colorful copy. You got no call to make trouble for me. It was you who started the scrap."

"I'll get over the scrap," I said, "in time. No grudges. You're making trouble for yourself. I just want some answers."

Without shifting a muscle he seemed to assume a crouch. His eyes regarded me balefully, reading a possibility of mayhem in my future.

"The camera story is pretty thin," I said.

"I don't give a damn! It's true. The truth is sometimes thin, ain't it?"

"Why didn't you pick up the camera before?"

"Geez," he said in disgust, "and you cops are supposed to be smart. In the first place, the Yamashitas were killed just three days ago. I knew them. I was shocked. I didn't think of the camera right away. When I did think about it and how I just had my word to prove it was mine, I came around here. The cops had the place staked out. I guess it was routine for them to keep an eye on the place until they picked up Nick Martin. Incidentally, lady," he said to Helen, "your husband sounded like a right guy who just had a wrong minute. I'm sorry about it."

Helen murmured a thanks.

Kuriacha lowered his compress and looked at his handkerchief. He seemed relieved that it showed no blood.

"When did you last see the Yamashitas?" I asked.

"Listen, you can't tie me into—"

"Let's not weary each other. Give me some more of that simple, direct action—a simple, direct answer."

He studied the .38 for a moment. "Well, I haven't seen Mrs. Yamashita in some time, maybe a month or more. She stayed home mostly. I saw Mr. Yamashita a week or ten days ago at his place of business. I stopped by there to go to lunch with Ichiro."

"Your friendship with Ichiro was your real connection with the family?"

"Mainly, I guess you could say. I liked the old folks, though. I never had a family. I liked them a lot."

"You counted Ichiro among your closest friends?"

"I don't know whether you could say that. We palled around together. He seemed to like to have me around, said I was colorful. He was always out for something different. Once at a party he'd bought some small horseshoes, the kind they put on ponies. He got me to twist them out of shape with my bare hands and gave them to his guests for souvenirs of the shindig. He got a charge out of stuff like that."

"I guess he had a string of women."

Kuriacha's face darkened. "Ichiro and his women is a long story, buster. I'm not acquainted with all the details. You'll have to get them someplace else."

"Jewels while he had a fancy to them, dirt when his fancy drifted?"

Kuriacha shrugged. "I told you, you'll have to ask somebody else."

"Any of them hate him enough to kill him?"

"Nick Martin killed him."

"Nick Martin is said to have killed Ichiro and his parents as well. As a matter of fact, Nick Martin didn't kill anybody."

"No?"

"Someone else went to the Yamashita summerhouse that afternoon."

"It ain't the way the paper reads."

"Newspapers revise from edition to edition. You watch later editions."

"Yeah? If you know so damn much, why don't you go to the cops and have Nick Martin released?"

"I'm still fishing."

"For what?"

"The identity of the person who went to the Yamashita house."

Kuriacha decided his recovery was well nigh complete. He got out of the chair, standing solidly on his bandy legs. "Well, I can't be baited, buster. I sure as hell didn't go out there and I don't know who did. Now you better put the popgun away. I'm going out of here and if you use it you'll find yourself in a lot of trouble."

With a beautifully direct simplicity, he turned his back and walked out of the apartment.

Helen looked at the closed door a moment. "Did you

mean what you said to him, Ed, about someone else going out to the Yamashita house that day?"

"Is Nick innocent?"

"Of course!"

"Then someone else had to go out there."

"With a—desire to kill three people?"

"That's the element creating the confusion," I said. "Dispose of it for a moment and you see the outlines of a different pattern, a fresh possibility. Someone went out there with no desire to harm the parents. He, or she, was after Ichiro."

"Yet the parents were killed."

"Because it was their misfortune to arrive while the murderer was still there. They had to be silenced."

"You can prove this, Ed?" she said, hope wild in her eyes.

"No. But the positions of the bodies, the way they were clothed when they were discovered, make me think I'm right."

"Then instead of a motive for a triple killing, you're looking for a motive for a single murder."

"Right. Ichiro's. Something he did sometime in his spotty past made someone want to kill him."

"Lord, Ed, he knew so many people, got around so much. Whatever he did might have been done in secret, known only to Ichiro and the person he did it to."

The brief flare of hope was gone from her eyes. I took her hand in both of mine and held her cold fingers for a moment.

"We'll think of one thing at a time," I said. "We'll keep chipping away. The way Nick would do."

She drew in a breath, held it for a moment. Then she said steadily, "Right."

CHAPTER **7** ▶ ▶ ▶ THE ABSENT-MINDED MEN with the bushy heads have a lot of theories about time and space. One thing is certain. The sweep of time is not an endless, smooth process to the person living it. There are stopped moments in time, moments frozen in a human brain.

It was that way with Helen Martin. As we got out of the rented heap on Caloosa Point, she stood with her brain seeing the gory scene again, the echo of a muffled scream inside of her.

I didn't rush her. I stood beside her until she was ready to walk from the car.

A hot, dead stillness lay over the Point. The water of the bay stretched heavy and turgid, like green-tinted glycerin under the crushing glare of the afternoon sun.

More than pocket change had been dropped on the Yamashita house. Made of California redwood and pastel brick, it sprawled comfortably and lazily behind its strip of private beach. A shift of the gaze brought into view the only other house on the Point, the white cottage Nick and Helen had leased for a summer's rental. It belonged to a northern businessman who used it only occasionally in the winter.

47

Fiddler crabs went rasping for their holes as we walked across the sizzling white sand.

Helen's fingers dug into my bicep as we approached the long gallery on the side of the Yamashita house.

"Here," she said, pointing.

The ghost of a dainty old lady was draped across the porch railing, her fingernails painted with blood.

We stepped upon the porch. From this point the other cottage down the beach was visible.

I stood where the unknown had stood, and the obvious question came to my mind. Had the people in that other cottage witnessed the violent moment?

Ichiro in a bedroom.

The little old man smashed down in the living room.

The silk-screen lady in headlong flight, screaming perhaps. She'd been trapped before she could get off the porch.

But she'd reached the open, and now the unknown stood with that question tearing at the mind.

Still carrying the bludgeon, the unknown ends the moment of hesitation. Nothing matters except survival—murder piled relentlessly upon murder, if that is the price.

I imagined the shadow, moving quickly across the distance separating the two houses. No faltering now. The bludgeon is ready.

The shadow falls across a doorway, across a sleeping man, a one-time killer of Japs. He has seen nothing, heard nothing.

The shadow turns to go. Turns back again. The sleeping man is like a gift. The samurai sword is on the wall. The whisky bottle is on the floor beside the sleeper.

In the sleeper there is safety.

The sword is lifted down. Nerves are steeled for the final act. The unknown recrosses to the Yamashita house. The sword does its work. The weapon is carried to the stand of mangrove crowding the inlet a hundred yards downbeach.

Insects begin to sing again over the marshy inlet. The heat shimmers. The day is silent. The shadow is gone.

I turned from my view of the white cottage, took out the steel, and opened the front door of the Yamashita house. The living room was long and cool. There were Japanese paintings on the walls, tables of ebony that might have been the work of Japanese craftsmen. Couches and chairs were arranged to provide an air of quiet, casual restfulness.

Helen and I turned into a hallway. The first bedroom had belonged to the parents—a big double bed, men's and women's garments in the closets.

Farther down the hallway was the bedroom where the chain reaction had begun.

A pair of Ichiro's slacks was thrown carelessly across a chair. His cigarettes and an initialed lighter were on the bedside table.

On the floor were chalk marks in the rough outline of a human body. He had been killed on the far side of the room, between the bed and the windows.

"We're going over this room a square inch at a time," I told Helen.

"What are we looking for, Ed, that the police might not have found already?"

"I don't know. You're a woman. I want you to look at it with a woman's eyes. Remember that it was a man's bedroom."

Thirty minutes later, I'd drawn a blank.

Helen hadn't.

I'd passed over the crumpled ball of pink tissue just as Steve Ivey had. It lay wadded in the heavy black glass ash tray on the bureau amid the butts and ashes.

With a feminine thoroughness, Helen picked up the small paper ball.

"Pink Kleenex," she said.

She blew the cigarette ash from it, and with delicate motions of her fingers opened up the ball.

Standing beside her, I saw the faint lipstick smudge on the tissue.

"Was she blonde or brunette, Helen?"

"From the little I can tell of the color of the lipstick," Helen said, "I'd guess she was blonde."

I folded the rumpled Kleenex and slipped it in my wallet. We went to the living room.

There were several pictures of Ichiro around. I passed up the one on the book shelf and chose a small, clear one that rested on a table in a gold frame. I opened the back of the frame, took out the picture, and dropped it in my pocket.

As I turned, I glanced out the window. A movement down near the mangrove caught my eye. He had been watching the house from there. He was hurrying away, quickly passing out of my line of vision.

I hadn't seen him clearly, but I was certain Prince Kuriacha had tailed us.

"Are we through here, Ed?"

"I think so."

"Then let's get away, please."

I took her arm and guided her out of the house. "You've been a trouper. I'm going to take you home now. I want you to rest."

I opened the car door for Helen. As I moved around the car I swept the landscape. There was no sign of Kuriacha.

I got in the car and we drove off. And the deathlike stillness returned to the Point.

It was a few minutes after six when I left Helen and returned downtown. I had a pint of beer and decided to eat later.

I walked around to Cass Street and entered the office building. The silence of it was broken only by a creak from the old girders and timbers, as some of the heat of the day seeped out.

It was a time for all good people to dine, relax, engage the evening.

I'd get my report out first.

I padded up the worn stairway. The building creaked. My office creaked.

I jerked my hand away from the doorknob and stood listening.

It sounded as if a very big rat were scuttling around in the office.

I put my palm on the .38 and stood to one side of the doorway. I heard the metallic sound of a file drawer being closed. Footsteps slipped softly to the door. The latch clicked.

When he opened the door, I heeled to face him, the .38 still in my pocket, my fingers around it.

He pulled up on his toes, his face turning to pearl-gray suède. He was thin, sallow, nervous, unhealthy looking. His long, bony fingers were deeply stained from his chain-smoking habits. His thin, drab, brown hair had receded until the fore part of his narrow pate was a scaly half moon of baldness.

His name was Sime Younkers. He was a debarred private detective. I knew his appearance to be deception at its best. He had the principles, endurance, and agility of a cottonmouth.

He stood staring at me with eyes the color of scrambled eggs.

"I was looking for you, Ed."

"I'll bet."

He made a move as if to close the door, reaching for the door with his right hand. It was his left hand that bothered me. I grabbed his left wrist, froze the hand in his pocket, and hit him in the face with my right fist.

He fell halfway across the office, tripped on his feet. A flare of pain lighted his face as he landed with his left arm twisted under him.

He pulled himself around. He sat up, holding his left shoulder, while blood seeped out of his thin nose.

I gripped the lapels of his coat and pushed the collar to his shoulders, forming a loose but effectively hampering restraint on his arms. The suit was a greasy Palm Beach, threadbare and smelling of old sweat. He sat unresisting.

I shook him down quickly. Whatever he'd copped from my file he'd put in his head, leaving the file so it would not arouse my suspicions.

I'd been wrong about his left hand. He was unarmed. He'd been reaching for a crumpled package of cigarettes. Being wrong didn't make me feel sorry.

"At least," I said, "you had sense enough to leave off the firearms with your license revoked."

"I didn't mean nothing, Ed. Honest."

"Sure," I said. "What did you find in the file?"

"Ed, I swear—"

"Now look, Sime. I've known you from away back. I don't like you. I don't like what your kind does to the profession. You'd pimp your own grandmother if there was a buck in it for you. The State of Florida was long suffering, Sime. You had to abuse your privileges repeatedly before your license was pulled. I'm not the State of Florida. I'm tired, hot, and hungry. I don't like the world in general right now and you in particular. Now what the hell were you doing in my files?"

"I came to see you, that's all. You're not in, see?

52

So I waited, and I got kind of curious, just idly curious, Ed."

"So I'm the State of Florida," I said. "One more chance, Sime."

"I'm telling you the truth."

"You just walked in the office, through a locked door."

"No. I got the janitor to let me in, Ed. I still got an old photostat of my license. I let him think what he would."

"You go through life asking for it, Sime."

"I got to get along, Ed. I got to eat. Man dies if he don't eat."

"You'll eat in Raiford, prison grub, you go around using that photostat to bully people. This is your last chance, Sime. The file, remember?"

"I didn't hook nothing, Ed. You searched me. Look in the file if you like. You won't find a thing gone. Just peeping, that's all."

I slapped his sore nose with the back of my hand.

"Ed," he said dismally, "you got no call to do that." He blinked the scrambled eggs at me. "You're like the rest of the world. I've tried hard, but I never had a break. It ain't my fault, Ed. See, I come here for a little help, and get a bust nose. Story of my life, that's all." He let the seepage of blood course around his mouth. A drop gathered on his pointed chin and fell to his dirty shirt. He seemed to be getting some kind of twisted pleasure from being a miserable spectacle.

"What kind of help?"

"I wanted to borrow a few bucks. I got a chance for a job, if I can get myself cleaned up and in shape."

"What kind of job?"

"Ain't I got no privacy at all?"

"Sure," I said. "The privacy of my office. You're lying all the way, Sime. You read the papers. You knew I was on the Yamashita case. There's a deep-down dirtiness behind the case. I'm not surprised to find the worms starting to crawl from the rot. Who sent you here?"

"I don't know what you're talking about," he said. His voice had gone sullen.

He sat waiting.

In his mind was something stronger than his fear of a beating.

"You've knocked off your chances like ducks in a shooting gallery," I told him. "That's your business. The Yamashita case is mine.

"Your chances are all used up, Sime. Nick Martin killed better men than you to keep this country decent and safe. You degrade what the Nick Martins did. You've taken what they gave you and befouled it.

"You're only a snake's belly above the person who would mutilate three bodies in order to frame Nick Martin. That's the ultimate befoulment of the deeds of the Nick Martins, Sime. I can't stomach it. I don't want to stomach it. So go back to that person and tell them I can't be bluffed, scared, or bought off. Then quit. Get out of it. Don't put any hurdles in my way—or I'll step on you the way I would a cockroach. Clear?"

"You got it all wrong, Ed," he muttered as he crabbed his way to the door. "I got nothing against a poor sucker like Nick Martin."

The toe of my shoe carried him into the hall. He was running before he got his full balance.

He went down the stair well like a crashing hod of bricks.

CHAPTER **8** ►►► "SORRY, ED," Steve Ivey said, rocking back behind his desk. "What you ask would keep my whole division busy. My boys are each capable of doing the work of three men, but not a dozen."

"The motive was in Ichiro's background," I said, for about the fifth time.

"Your supposition. What have you given me? Martin's story about the house slippers. A professional wrestler entering Ichiro's apartment. A smudge of lipstick on a Kleenex. Sime Younkers' appearance in your office. Where's your concrete evidence?"

The fluorescent lighting in his office gave Ivey's face a pale look. "Don't ride me, Ed. You've been a cop. You know what it's like. You live in a dirty world apart, with death around the next corner or on the next call. We're supposed to work an eight-hour day. We're on call twenty-four. To be cops, we've had to turn our backs on the hope of ever making any real money. We, and every department in the country, stagger under a work load that would drive us nuts if we stopped to think about it. Joe Citizen likes to bawl us out and remind us we're public servants if we catch him running a red light. The same Joe wants us to materialize, fearless and almighty and ready to spill our blood for his sake, if he hollers for help. It's nearly four-

55

teen hours since I started this tour of duty, and the murders, muggings, and rapes haven't stopped. So don't ride me."

"Sorry."

"Damn it, I can't stop everything else and pick Ichiro's life to pieces, moment by moment, because you've got an idea in your hard head."

He rocked forward and slapped his desk with his palm. "Sit down and quit looking like you want to tear something up. That is, if you want to hear what I can do and am doing."

For answer, I took the chair across the desk from him.

He eyed me for a moment. "I said I couldn't do what you asked. I didn't say I wouldn't like to. My orders come from higher up. From people who are certain of Nick Martin's guilt and eventual conviction. How long would I last if I ignored the orders, the pressure of the masses of other work, and kept this division on the Martin case?"

"About five minutes," I said.

"Right. I'm keeping Figueroa's time as free as possible from other work. I'm curious myself to know where Ichiro was a few hours before his death."

"Why?"

"A human hair. A long, blond hair." He lifted his hands and massaged his neck briefly. "Let's take it from point of beginning. When Ichiro's body was brought in, the pathologist noticed the hair. It was twined around Ichiro's right arm, tangled with the short, dark body hair. The detail was odd enough to strike a spark of curiosity. The pathologist 'scoped the hair. The cellular structure was strange enough to cause him to take a second look."

"Strange in what way?"

"The hair," Ivey said, "had every appearance of having come from the head of a long-dead person, a corpse."

Ivey's wry grin told me I had a dumb look on my face. "I'm only telling you," he said, "what the pathologist told me. He wouldn't guarantee his finding. He said only that the hair had that appearance."

The phone skirled on Ivey's desk. He picked it up. I vaguely heard the two-way conversation. Ivey gave an order to bring somebody in and hung up.

"Punk kid broke," he said. "We know where some of our present supply of marijuana is coming from."

"Yeah?"

"Little white-haired woman growing it," Ivey said. "In rows of boxes on the roof of a slum tenement in West Tampa."

Ivey growled as the phone commanded attention again. He picked it up.

It seemed a *bolita* numbers runner had used a straight razor on his mistress. She was alive, in a hospital. She'd never be pretty again, unless by some miracle she could afford the best in plastic surgeons. A manhunt was on, with a thousand dark holes to shelter the numbers runner.

All in a day's work for Ivey.

I decided to go home and sleep on the thought of a blond hair, courtesy of a corpse.

Slide over to early evening, the next day. The day wouldn't have interested you. I cooled my feet waiting to see people; then blistered them again going to see other people—a probate judge I knew, a banking official, a secretary in the firm of Cameron and Yamashita, a customer of the same firm, a newsstand operator in the lobby of the building where the firm had its offices, the credit manager of the city's ritziest men's-wear store.

I learned that no blonde woman, alive or deceased, was or had been employed by Cameron and Yamashita. Ichiro

57

had put in a short working day, but when he'd worked, he'd been good at it. His mind had been keen, his grasp of detail thorough; his business personality had sparkled. He'd been a real asset to the firm.

His financial affairs had been in reasonable order. He had made no sudden, large expenditures before his death, and he hadn't borrowed any large sums. In his off-business hours he had rioted through a respectable income to the final penny, but he had kept his bills current.

I got back to the apartment with my shirt sweat-plastered to my back and my socks feeling like layers of hot grease. I soaked until the water in the tub felt tepid, dressed, and cooked a dinner of pork and beans and Cuban sausage on the gas burner. I was pushing out the inner wrinkles with the food and icy beer when somebody knocked on the door.

Crossing the bed-sitting room, I swung the door wide.

Rachie Cameron was standing in the gloomy hallway. She was wearing a skirt, and a blouse cut in straight lines like a short smock with a loose drawstring neck. The smoothness of her tanned cheeks was flushed. Her short, dark hair was a little disheveled.

"Hi, ugly man."

"What brings you to this neighborhood?"

For answer, she looked me up and down, little pin-points of light sparking in her eyes.

Her grin was more a sullen pout. "Aren't you going to ask me in?"

"Sure."

She let her loose, careless walk carry her into the apartment. As she passed close, I inhaled a deep breath. If she'd been drinking, I couldn't smell it.

I closed the door and watched her survey the apartment. "Just like I pictured it," she said, as if something had pleased her.

She was carrying a large straw handbag. She took out a cigarette, lighted it, and dropped the handbag on the day bed.

Her passage to the kitchenette doorway was leisurely. "I'm starved," she said.

"Sit down and help yourself."

She got acquainted with the kitchenette quickly, filling a plate and sitting across the table from me.

"Beer?" I asked.

"Uh huh."

I got her a can of beer, opened it, and handed it to her.

"I'm glad you didn't put it in a glass," she said.

"Yeah?"

"It would have been out of character. I'll bet you don't act out of character often."

"I don't know," I said. "I don't spend much time analyzing myself."

"It's because you're not all mixed up. You know who you are."

She ate quickly, hungrily. With a crust of bread she scooped bean sauce from her plate.

When she had gone through the rough grub, she lit another cigarette, propped her elbows on the table, and sat sipping her beer and smoking. "Can I fix you something else, Ed?"

"No, thanks. How about yourself?"

"Had plenty."

I shoved the chair back and started to pick up the dishes.

"You're not going to bother with those now, are you?" she asked.

"I'd thought about it."

"Let them go. A few dirty dishes won't hurt anything."

She stood up, gathered the things, and made a piled-up

59

mess of the sink. Then she went into the bed-sitting room and sat on the day bed with her feet tucked under her. She smoked and let the ashes dribble on the floor. With a contented stretch, she leaned the back of her head and shoulders against the wall.

She acted as if the apartment were a natural habitat where she had been a long time and which she had no intention of leaving.

"You're a long way from Davis Islands," I said.

"Those damned prisses!"

"Your father know where you are?"

"Why should he? I'm a quarter-century old, ugly man. I quit taking orders from that jerk a long time ago."

"You're a very good-looking girl."

"I'm glad you think so."

"You didn't let me finish. I was going to say that most girls of your age and looks are married."

"Ninnies," she said.

I moved near the day bed, to the table that held the telephone. She uncoiled and stood up.

I picked up the phone, and she said, "What are you doing?"

"I think your father should know where you are."

"I won't have him coming here after me! I won't!"

I had the phone half-raised to my ear. She grabbed the cord and jerked the phone out of my hand. It struck the floor. When I bent and reached for it, she tried to beat me to it.

I shoved her back a couple of feet and tried to hold her off with my free hand.

She uttered an unladylike word, freed herself, and made another try at the phone. She got her hands on it and tried to yank it from my ear.

Her hand slipped. Her nails left a stinging red furrow

down the side of my face. As I put the phone down slowly, she backed off a step or two.

All the boredom was gone from her now. The vacant film had vanished from the surface of her dark eyes. Her breath quickened.

"You're bleeding, Ed."

"I know."

"I didn't mean to do it. Let me fix it up for you."

She darted into the bathroom, clicked the light on. I heard her rummaging in the medicine cabinet. She sounded as if she were taking stuff out at random, making a mess, putting nothing back.

She came out carrying a bottle of after-shave lotion.

"The Merthiolate would leave your face all marked. This will do just as well."

She stood close to me, pouring a few drops of the lotion in her hand. She patted the fingernail marks.

"Does it sting, Ed?"

"A little."

"You wouldn't mind a little hurt like that. It would take a real hurt to flatten a man like you, wouldn't it?"

"I've been flattened," I said.

The movement of her fingers slowed. They rested, lingering against my cheek.

She dropped the shave-lotion bottle on the table. Her other hand rose. The back of her knuckles brushed the hard, late-in-the-day stubble on my jowl.

"Don't throw me out, Ed," she pleaded softly. "I've thought of nothing but you since you came to the house. You don't know what it's like, the dullness, the monotony, the boredom that strangles you until you think you'll scream."

She was young and beautiful. I'm a man and therefore not immune. Then I saw the receding depths of her

61

eyes and unpleasant, tiny spider feet slipped up and down my spine.

I gripped her wrists and pushed her away from me.

"You don't need me," I said. "What you need is a good spanking or something to interest you enough to cause you to put in a few hard days of work."

"Go ahead and be mean to me," she said, suddenly sullen.

"I think you'd enjoy it if I did," I told her. "But get one thing straight, Rachie. You're no dice with me."

"You're just saying that."

"Good night, Rachie."

"I won't go home!" she threatened. "I'll go out and do something desperate."

"Maybe your father will pick up the pieces."

"You wouldn't care a bit, would you?"

"Well, you're a quarter-century old."

Her demeanor and voice underwent another of those quick changes. "Couldn't I make you care just a little, Ed? You're being mean and brutal, you know."

"Sorry."

"You're treating me like this because you know I can't strike back."

"And you're having fun, a break in that streak of boredom. But I haven't any more time. I've got work to do."

CHAPTER **9** ▶▶▶ "WORK?" she said.

"That's right. You can look the word up in the dictionary sometime."

"Are you still fooling around with that Yamashita thing?"

62

"Still trying, Rachie."

"They were icky"—she curled her nose—"except for Ichiro."

I didn't permit myself to glance at her. "I guess you miss the good times you and Ichiro had."

"I said he was passable. I didn't say he was charged."

"Still, he's gone."

"Everything ends," she said. "Why think about it?"

"I imagine your father would have wanted someone more stable for you."

"Ordinarily he'd have given a cat like Ichiro the boot."

"Ordinarily?"

"He didn't try to examine Ichiro too closely." A sneer touched her voice. "Money involved, you know. Yamashita had the controlling interest in the firm."

"When did you last see Ichiro?"

"The day that he died." She grinned at me. "That gave you a start, didn't it?"

"How long before he died?"

"Really"—she tossed her head—"I think we've talked about it enough. Let's talk about you and me some more."

"Quit asking for me to slap it out of you, Rachie. I'll take the other alternative and let the cops talk to you."

"About Ichiro?"

"What else?"

"Oh, be immovable, you big, ugly cluck! You stink of sweat anyway."

"Ichiro," I said, an edge in my voice.

"He came by my house the day he was killed. Wanted to know if I was going on a yachting party the next day, Sunday. That's all there was to it. Are you satisfied?"

"What time was it?"

"Afternoon."

"He say anything about how he was going to spend the rest of the day?"

63

"Nope. He had the fidgets. I gathered he was going to meet somebody."

"Where?"

"How should I know? Next thing I heard of him, he'd been killed at the Yamashita beach house a few hours later." She put her hands on her hips and tilted her head. "You know, maybe I got my wires crossed about you. Maybe, after all, you're just a square, inhibited, puritanical cluck." She giggled. "And all the time I was thinking of you the way some of the creamy women of ancient Rome must have thought of the big barbarians who came sweeping out of the north."

"We were talking about Ichiro."

"Yes, and I'm bored."

"Jail would be a lot more boring."

"How could you put me in jail?"

"On a charge of soliciting," I said. "All I have to do is pick up the phone."

"Great," she said with enthusiasm. "Sounds like a real diversion. Go ahead and call your cops, Ed."

I stood fingering the lobe of my ear. No wonder Victor Cameron was gray with defeat.

Mentally, I sighed.

Then I slapped the hell out of her.

She fell against the day bed and half-lay, her arm supporting her, her skirt tight about her knees. She held her reddened cheek, and I said, "You ever see Ichiro with a blonde woman?"

"Yes, Ed."

"When?"

"Two times, I think."

"He bring her to parties?"

"No, he was alone with her both times. I just happened to see him. Once, driving with her in his car, the second time in a restaurant one night."

"Who was she?"

"I don't know. Honest, I don't."

"Did anything happen to her?"

"In what way?"

"Did she die or get killed?"

"Not that I know of."

She sat up and looked at me meekly. "Why do you ask a question like that, Ed?"

"I was thinking of a hair from a dead woman's head," I said.

"I don't understand."

"You don't need to."

"Yes, Ed."

"Would you know this woman if you saw her again?"

"Isn't she dead? You just said—"

"In the event she's still alive, would you recognize her?"

"I think so."

"You know the places Ichiro frequented?"

"Some of them."

"Fine. Go powder your nose and comb your hair. We're going out. To some joints."

"Yes, Ed."

We went from the sibilant rattlesnake rasp of maracas to the neurotic wailing of an alto sax to the frenzied throb of Dixieland drums. From a tiny cellar club in Ybor City to the penthouse club in a fine hotel. In every smoky hole we looked at blondes, all shapes and sizes, from bleached, leathery-faced sluts to pretty, vapid, misty young things. I had the small, clear picture of Ichiro which I'd copped from the Yamashita summerhouse. One by one, managers, waiters, bus boys shook their heads. Whether they'd known the pictured man or not, the answer was the same. None remembered him in the company of a blonde.

65

The night indicated that the blonde for whom we were looking didn't exist.

But a ball game isn't finished in the first inning. I knew she did exist, alive or dead.

She had existed for Ichiro, but for some reason he had hidden her existence with care. The possible number of reasons offered a big, new headache. She might have been respectably married. Or hiding from something, afraid. Or staying under cover because she was part of a thing Ichiro didn't want broadcast from the rooftops, a thing he was planning or a thing he'd already done. Or it could be the other way, and Ichiro could have been part of a thing *she* didn't want broadcast.

Maybe the reason for the discretion had brought them together. Again, the opposite could be true, with the reason developing only because their lives had come together.

Three A.M. The heat lay sticky over the city and a mist rose like the breath of a torpid swamp as I drove the rented car across the Hillsborough River.

I took Bayshore Boulevard, and when I turned off on the spur and bridge that led to Davis Islands, Rachie said, "I don't want to go home."

"It's late."

"Oh, no. It's early. Nice and early in the morning. I'm just getting my energy up."

"Well," I said, "you can swim it off when you get home."

Her breath hissed at me. I felt her eyes, angry and hot with rebellion, study my face in the dim glow of the dash lamp.

She decided I meant what I said.

When I braked the car in front of her house, she slammed the door open. "Now I know."

"Do you?"

"Sure. My first impression was all wrong. You're a washed-out, tired old man."

"I'm glad you understand."

"I don't care if I never see you again."

"Good night, Rachie."

"You go to the devil!"

I waited until she was inside the house. As I reached for the ignition key, a male voice said, "Rivers."

He came from the shrubbery lining the driveway. In the wan moonlight, his face was the gray ghost of a face that had belonged to a one-time man who'd called himself Victor Cameron.

His slow steps carried him the short distance to my side of the car.

"I was waiting up," he said. "I saw the headlights of the car and had time to step behind the shrubs."

I waited.

"You've had her out a long time, Rivers," he said.

"I didn't ask her out."

"I guess not," he said heavily. He wiped the back of his hand across his face. "But the rest of us—we have a responsibility for a person like her."

"I brought her home unsullied, if that's what you're asking."

"Thanks," he said. "Do me a favor, Rivers, and stay away from her."

"You do me one," I said, "and keep her away from me."

He looked at me dully. Then he turned toward the house, moving with the attitude of a man whose flesh can repeat a long journey but whose spirit cannot.

Later, stretched in my shorts while my sweat puddled the day bed, I forgot Victor Cameron and sick daughter. I wondered if Nick Martin were sleeping. Nights, sometimes, were when pain came slipping through the hell gates war had opened in his flesh.

Marvel as I might at his endurance and self-mastery, I knew that each passing hour without some word of hope brought the final breaking point that much nearer.

Nick had managed to remain a relative stranger to self-pity, regret, bitterness. But no man is shut alone in a cell. He's caged by more than steel. He's trapped in a timeless void with all the shadows he's accumulated during his life.

If Nick was to be helped, it must be soon.

CHAPTER **10** ▶ ▶ ▶ THERE ARE about a million people in the Greater Tampa Bay area. They work in stores, offices, or the light, airy, air-conditioned, smokeless factories industrial commissions have wooed to Florida. They play in water that sparks with frosty phosphorescence at night, on white beaches where the sand is as fine as talc, in cool cocktail lounges and pastel stucco and glass homes. The dregs among the million live in a squalor and filth Mr. Average American is likely to associate with the backward areas of Puerto Rico or Mexico, but never with the rich, well-fed giant of the United States.

I had to believe that one among the million was a blonde woman who could give me some answers I needed.

I'd never seen her. I had no description of her. I didn't know if she was alive or dead, where she had come from, or what her name might be.

I was out early. A brief call to police headquarters got me names of a few of Ichiro's friends. From these I learned the identity of other people he'd known. I talked to thirty or forty people that day. Among them were blonde women, but not the right one. Not a blonde who'd been careful never to be seen openly with Ichiro.

He'd had a few friends in Sarasota, the ritzy coastal playground a few miles south of Tampa.

I'd try Sarasota tomorrow.

I drove the rented car to my apartment building and parked on the street. The agency hires its cars on an annual rate from a nationwide auto-rental firm. That way we have a new car every year, no worries with gas, oil, tires, upkeep. What with taxes and the simplicity of the setup, we come out all right, with no additional details to clutter our operations.

It was late afternoon, the sun a fiery red ball poised for its plunge into the Gulf.

A gang of kids chattering in Spanish came racing down the sidewalk. They were ragged, unkempt, as brown as seasoned walnut, and as healthy as stringy mongrel pups that have had to learn a little savagery.

I lumbered up to the apartment, started cold water in the tub, and opened a pint can of beer.

I sat at the kitchenette table with the beer for a few moments to let some of the hard, steady pumping go out of my feet. I looked from the window at the dirty roof-tops jammed together. On south, away from the jamming and ugliness, lay Sarasota.

Nick's last chance?

It could well be.

If I found her there, I knew what I would say. I wouldn't take long in saying it. She'd better not take long in giving some straight answers, if she valued her health.

And then suddenly the doubt became overpowering, building itself into a certainty that she wouldn't be found in Sarasota. There was no reason for her to be. Ichiro

69

had few friends there. Those had formerly resided in Tampa. He had gone to Sarasota very infrequently and his stays had never been long. His interests and just about every hour of his life had been centered in Tampa. The chance that he had met the blonde in Sarasota was too slim to build hope on.

Where then?

In Tampa, his center post.

How? Not at a party. I'd have got some kind of hint of that from someone among thirty or forty people interviewed. Not at a night spot; they hadn't been seen together in night spots.

Without breaking my chain of thought, I wandered to the bathroom and turned off the cold tap.

There was a click in my mental gears, and I was shaken because I'd overlooked the obvious. The odds were not a million to one. They were a million to two.

There had to be a second person. The person who had introduced Ichiro and the blonde, who'd brought them together. Unless you wanted to believe that Ichiro and the woman had met entirely by accident, introducing themselves, forming a friendship, with no one else present.

Think about the second person for a moment. Man or woman? No way of knowing yet. Friend of Ichiro's? Unlikely, unless they were all good liars.

If not a friend, what would motivate the second person to introduce the blonde to Ichiro?

And what would springboard Ichiro? He was a sensualist, seeker after pleasure, partaker of the erotic, searcher for thrills.

I wheeled into the bedroom. There was a black notebook in the drawer of the telephone table. I thumbed it open, flipped a page, found a name and phone number.

Sweat gathered in a heavy drop on the end of my nose. I brushed it off, picked up the phone, and dialed. It rang about six times. I'd about decided she was out when Tillie Rollo answered. She had a pleasant, smooth voice softened with culture.

"Ed Rivers, Tillie."

"How are you?"

"Busy."

"Yes, I noticed your name in the newspapers."

"Any of the other names mean anything to you?"

"Do you have a particular name in mind?" she asked.

"Ichiro Yamashita."

There was a pause. "Perhaps," she said.

"Fine. I've got a question—"

"My hairdresser is here, Ed. I'm very busy. Why don't you drop out a little later and we'll have a glass of sherry."

"What time?"

"In an hour or so."

"I'll be there," I said.

I dunked my bulk, put on some fresh clothes, went to the corner restaurant and ate some chicken and yellow rice.

Then I picked up the rented heap and drove out to see Tillie.

She lived in a good section of town in a very comfortable home made of adobe bricks and rustic siding. The lawn and shrubbery had been meticulously tended. A foreign-built sport car stood in the driveway near the carport.

There was no red light over Tillie's front door.

The chimes sounded softly, and she opened the door immediately. She was a very good-looking young woman. She wore her copper-red hair in an upsweep. Her eyes were green and cool, her complexion like ivory-colored satin. Her dress was a quiet blue in excellent taste.

"You're very prompt," she said, as she stepped aside for me to enter.

71

The interior of the house was airy and cool, furnished simply and comfortably. There was nothing crude or blatant about Tillie. The only tool of her trade on the premises was the pastel-blue telephone in a small alcove off the living room. No girl ever came here—she was required to keep her own apartment or cottage, buy her own clothes—and govern her life by instructions given over the pale-blue telephone. If she failed in any of these requirements, she found life exceptionally difficult for her in Tampa.

"Have you had dinner, Ed?"

"Yes, thanks."

"Would you care for a drink?"

"No, thanks."

Tillie crossed the room and sat in a tapestry-covered wing chair. She sat midway in the seat, her back very straight, her knees neatly together, her hands folded in her lap. She looked like a member of the Junior League on her best behavior.

"Shall we quit sparring around, Ed?"

"Let's."

"You know about the girl Ichiro Yamashita saw the day of his death, of course."

"That's why I called," I said.

"Yes, I'm not exactly stupid, Ed. You're wrong, however. The girl had nothing to do with what happened on Caloosa Point. The affair has been cleared up to the satisfaction of the police. The guilty man is in jail."

I'd taken the chair she'd indicated. Now I leaned forward slightly. "Tillie, in the dictates of your own code, you've always walked carefully, never indulging in double-dealing."

"My honesty and fairness have never been questioned. I don't feel I've done anything wrong. I deal in a commodity. I find there are growing numbers of sellers and

72

buyers, a factor over which I have no control. The market is active, but I didn't create it. I'm not responsible for the tenor of the times, Ed."

Looking at the calm, poised beauty of Tillie Rollo, I shuddered inside. I hoped it didn't show.

"What is it you're driving at, Ed?"

"I want a favor."

"Why should I do you a favor?"

"Because I'm going to do you one," I said. "The police are not completely satisfied. Steve Ivey still has one man assigned to the case."

The emerald of her eyes darkened. "It hasn't been in the papers."

"That's a silly remark, coming from you, Tillie."

"I suppose so. I've heard from reliable sources that you're absolutely a man of your word. I don't think you're trying to scare me."

"If I wanted to do that," I said, "I'd pick a more effective method."

She sat thoughtful. "Does it appear I'm in for much unpleasantness?"

"That depends a lot on you."

"Any publicity would be dreadful. There is no such thing as favorable publicity in my business."

She looked at me gravely. "Ed, I need your help. I must have it."

"I'll do what I can."

"It's imperative that I stay officially clean. My name has never been in the newspapers or on a police blotter. I can't have a thing like that following me."

"You planning on going somewhere?" I asked.

"I live only for the day when I'll go. All this"—she made a vague motion with her hand—"this life is only a transitory thing, like a dream, not quite real to me. Reality will begin when it's all over."

73

"You could get out any time, Tillie."

"No," she said tightly, "it's not that simple. You don't understand."

"Anybody got a gun at your head?"

"Of course not. But I won't settle for anything less than everything I have in mind."

"And what do you have in mind?"

"I'm going to be a lady," she said.

"I see."

"No you don't! You think you do, but there are so many things you don't know. I grew up hating poverty. It was the one real, crushing thing in my life. You see, my parents were the end products of a way of life that had vanished forever. They never could quite cope with themselves or circumstances. My mother died while I was still in school, and my father drank himself to death.

"I wonder where he got the money for the alcohol. We lived in the remains of an old mansion in South Carolina. I was taught all the niceties, trained to be a lady, in a home where holes in the roof permitted the rains to stain the portraits of the aristocratic dead ones we called our forebears.

"I could speak a little French by the time I was thirteen. I knew a bit of classical literature from the moldering volumes in our home. My mother tutored me in the manners of a lady, even if there were only cowpeas on the table.

"I was the odd chick in a flock of well-fed neighboring farm children, a laughingstock. At times, I hated my mother almost as much as the children for her helplessness, her fragile, bewildered inability to stop going through motions that bore no resemblance to reality.

"A long time ago I made up my mind. There was only one thing I could do. Go ahead and be a lady.

"All I needed was money. Soon now I'll have enough.

One day I won't be in Tampa any longer. No one will know where I've gone or what name I'll be carrying. It's a big country, Ed. In some far corner I'll find a nice little town tucked away. I'll settle there. I'll meet only the best people. I'll entertain most properly and bring them to me. In that town there will be a man. He'll be respectable and substantial. I'll find him. I'll marry him. And I'll spend the rest of my days presiding over the best social circle in that little town. It may sound dull and stuffy to a lot of people, but it's what I want and what I intend to have—the reason my picture must never be in an official file."

She had grasped the arms of the wing chair in increasing intensity as she talked. Now she relaxed and sat looking at me as if disconcerted by the violence of feeling inside of herself.

"Who was the girl, Tillie?"

"I'm bargaining," she said tautly.

"I can't speak for the police," I said. "I'll promise you all that I can—and that is to point out to Steve Ivey that you've helped. If you do help."

"I want something more than that."

I stood up. "Then I guess you'll have to deal with the police directly."

"Wait!" she said. "I suppose I'll have to take the best offer I can get."

"That's right."

"The girl's name is Luisa Shaw."

"That means nothing to me. Where is she now?"

"I don't know."

"You keep track of them, don't you?" I asked.

"Yes, but she's moved. I tried to find her. She was living in a motel near the bay. Gave no notice. Left no forwarding address. Simply vanished."

"When?"

"I don't know exactly."

75

"What did she look like?"

"Blonde. Long, blonde hair. Teasing sort of face. Small, lively figure. A really beautiful girl. Almost hauntingly beautiful," Tillie said.

"Hauntingly?"

"Something inside of her—a kind of morbid fascination for what she was doing."

"When did you see her last, Tillie?"

"I saw her only the one time, the night she came here. They usually have a hard time getting to me and have to be referred by someone I know. I mistrusted her at first. There is always the possibility of a policewoman plant."

"What made you start trusting her?"

"Ichiro Yamashita called. I gave him her number. I knew I could trust Ichiro."

"You must have known him well," I said.

"Yes."

"You don't sound as if you liked him."

"I despised him. I despised them all, Ed. They're only a means to that little town with its single country club and small group that really counts."

"Ichiro call you the day he was killed?"

"Luisa Shaw called me the day before," Tillie said. "She was to meet Ichiro at the Yamashita summerhouse. The parents were to have dinner out. She and Ichiro would dine in the summerhouse and go to a small, card-admittance club for the evening."

"Neatly laid plans," I commented. "Luisa Shaw always kept you posted?"

"She proved to be the most trustworthy of the lot. Always mailed my share of the money to me. Plain envelope. Cash. I never had to send anyone around to keep tabs on her or collect."

I stood mulling it over. Then I said, "Do you know Rachie Cameron, Tillie?"

"Not personally. Only by reputation. Ichiro used to speak of her sometimes."

"Used to? His relationship with Rachie changed after he met Luisa Shaw?"

"Come to think of it," Tillie mused, "he hadn't mentioned Rachie Cameron recently." She studied me carefully. "What are you driving at?"

"Jealousy," I said, "bubbling in an undisciplined, sick brain."

Tillie stared at me, going pale. "You mean . . ."

"I don't mean anything," I said, "as yet. I'm only pointing out that if one unknown person went to the Yamashita summerhouse, that two might have."

"But Rachie Cameron—a slip of a girl."

"Lithe, athletic," I said.

"But these people—"

"One to start with. Ichiro. Then the parents walk in. Ichiro was dissipated, probably had the strength of a bowl of mush. The parents were old. The vigorous strength of youth would have been sufficient."

"You frighten me, Ed!"

"I'm sorry."

"So like a battle-scarred old bulldog with a strain of wolf. Use a little of that in my behalf, will you?"

"I'll keep my word to you," I said.

"I'm counting on you, Ed."

"I'll do for you exactly what I promised," I told her, a harshness in my voice.

I needed to get away from the ladylike niceness of the thing here in the center of its web.

It had grown dark outside while I'd talked with Tillie. I started down the walk, and he came from a concealing shrub.

The barbered grass deadened his footsteps. I knew he was there when the massive forearm chin-locked me from behind and the knee nearly ruptured the end of my spine.

I was held rigid. I couldn't see the bandy-legged bulk in the natty clothes, or the pear-shaped, hairless gorilla face. But I felt Prince Kuriacha's breath on the back of my neck and recognized the guttural voice quickly enough.

"You mind your business," he said. "Ain't you got any respect for the dead? You leave the Yamashitas alone."

The explosion in my tail bone had eased to the activity of a few small, intermittent firecrackers.

"Why?" I said.

"The guilty man is in jail."

"That the only reason?"

The grip didn't loosen. "They were my friends," Kuriacha said. "When I was a poverty-stricken bum with nothing to eat in California, Sadao's brothers were kind to me. Even if it wasn't the old man doing it himself, on account of he wasn't there, I don't forget easy. So lay off, wise guy. I ain't having you throw dirt all over the Yamashita name."

He thought I was properly cowed. He turned me loose and stepped back.

I faced him slowly, my hands on my neck, the palms working at the muscles.

His glower was intended to let me know he wasn't kidding.

He was a wrestler.

I wasn't.

I hit him in the face hard enough to break the bone. He took the blow on the granite of his cheek. A low-pitched roar came out of him. Arms opened wide, he lunged at me.

If he ever got those arms on me, he could kill me.

I feinted him to one side and hit him again. This time he sat down on the grass with blood pouring from his nose.

"The odds should be about even if we ever meet for the rubber match," I told him.

His muscles quivered. He seemed on the point of gathering himself to spring.

"You do it," I said, "and you'll be digesting your teeth."

The stalemate held while I backed away and he sat perfectly still.

CHAPTER **11** ▶ ▶ ▶ I PHONED Helen Martin that evening. She answered the pay phone outside her apartment door quickly. Her hello was taut, too anxious. The years of mountainous misfortune hadn't broken her. But this waiting alone near a telephone was severing her endurance a thread at a time.

"Don't get your hopes up," I said, "but I'm seeing Steve Ivey tomorrow morning."

"You have something, Ed?"

"I know the identity of the person who went to the Yamashita cottage the day of the killings. A blonde call girl known as Luisa Shaw. She operated for a silky madam named Tillie Rollo. Either name mean anything to you?"

"No. Ed, does it mean that she, this Luisa Shaw . . ."

"There is nothing to indicate that she was anything other than innocent—of murder, at least. But I'm going to use it all I can as a lever on Ivey."

"Ed, it must work. I don't think I could stand another disappointment."

79

"Cut out that kind of talk, Helen. I know it's tough. Get out of the apartment for a little while."

"No. I couldn't stand crowds of free people, open space. Always before the loneliness had a grain of hope in it, that Nick would get out of the hospital again soon and feel better. It's never been like this."

"Want me to come over and yak at you awhile?"

"I'd rather be alone, Ed. Bright chatter would only be a pretense."

"Get yourself a good dinner and a night's sleep. I'm counting on you, Helen. So is Nick."

"I will," she said. "I have some sleeping pills. Maybe I'll feel better tomorrow."

"Sure you will."

"I'll be right by the telephone, and I'm keeping a radio on the newscasts."

"Just give me some time," I said. "We haven't had a setback yet."

"Sure, Ed. Do you know how to get hold of this Luisa Shaw?"

"No," I said. "She moved. Left no trace. Even the madam couldn't find her, and the madam is pretty thorough in that sort of thing. This is favorable to us, this appearance her flight has created. Do you see?"

"Yes, Ed."

"Ivey may have something on her. Tomorrow may tell a different story."

Tomorrow . . .

I saw Sime Younkers coming out of headquarters when I approached the building. He saw me at the same moment, turned his head, and ducked quickly into the sidewalk crowd.

Wondering what the disbarred private eye had wanted here, I entered the building and went to Ivey's office.

80

The lieutenant wasn't in. I cooled my heels for ten minutes or so, and then he arrived.

He arrived with his heel kicking the door closed, with a steel-trap look about his mouth and a dark cloud swathing his face.

"Somebody steal your promotion, Ivey?"

"Oh, hello, Ed. No, a green man let Sime Younkers go up to talk to Nick Martin. I don't like that crumb Younkers in the same county with me. I don't like him fooling around my prisoners, trying to sell them any bills of goods. What's on your mind, anyway?"

"I've got a piece of news for you."

"Yeah?"

"I know who went out to the Yamashita summerhouse the day they were killed."

He jerked his head toward me. His mind dropped everything else.

"Her name is Luisa Shaw," I said. "Call girl."

"Never heard of her. How do you know she went out there?"

"She had an appointment, with Ichiro Yamashita."

"Who says so?"

"I made a halfway bargain with my source, Ivey."

He thought it over, looking at me and fingering his lower lip. Then he moved to his desk and sat down. Sunlight from behind him sparkled on his bald head.

Flipping a button on his intercom, Ivey gave a couple of orders.

We waited.

A tall young man in the lightweight, dark shirt and trousers, summer uniform of the Tampa police, entered the office.

Ivey looked at the cop's empty hands. "Nothing, Baxter?"

"Not a thing, sir. She's never been picked up in Tampa."

"File of known prostitutes?"

"Not there either, sir."

"She could have changed her name," I said.

"You want to look at pictures for a while?" Ivey asked.

I shook my head. "Mug views wouldn't help. I don't know what she looks like."

"Where does she live?"

"I don't know."

"You don't know a hell of a lot, Rivers, to be so sure she went to the Yamashita house that day."

The intercom rasped for Ivey's attention. He pushed a button down. "Yes?"

The intercom gave the voice a hollow, tinny sound. "Lieutenant, Nick Martin has sent down word that he wants to see you."

"What about?"

"He didn't say. He requested that you see him immediately. Said it's important."

"I'll go right up," Ivey said, clicking off the intercom.

Without invitation, I dogged his heels out of the office. Nick stood quietly in his cell. It seemed to me there were a few new lines etched in his face, tentacles of a weariness smothering the very soul of the man. The pale, fair skin had developed faint blue shadows under the eyes. His short-cut blond hair looked limp, lifeless. The slight remains of the boyishness of his features were a mockery.

Calmly, he said hello to Ivey and me. He looked at me with regret heavy in his eyes. "Ed, I appreciate everything you've tried to do."

"I'm still swinging," I said.

"Is Helen all right?"

"Sure," I said.

The jailer locked the cell door behind us. Nick went over and eased himself onto the edge of the iron bunk. Ivey stood near the cell door.

"You wanted to see me?" Ivey asked.

"Yes," Nick said.

"What's on your mind?"

"I want to settle the issue."

"I'm listening," Ivey said.

Nick looked unseeingly at the big, squarish hands resting on his knees. Without raising his eyes, he said, "I killed them."

Ivey glanced at me. "I see. You understand, Martin, that you asked for me to listen to you, that you are doing this voluntarily, that it will be used against you."

"I understand," Nick said.

"I'll get it taken down," Ivey said, "and you can sign it."

Nick said nothing for a few seconds. When he raised his head, I, not Ivey, received his attention.

"Well, Ed?"

"Well, what?"

"You haven't said anything. Just stood there."

"He no longer has an interest in the case," Ivey said. "How come you decided to confess, Martin?"

"I remember now," Nick said, "It came back—like in a dream."

"And the house slippers?"

"Weak alibi," Nick said dully.

"Nick," I said, "you're a liar."

Ivey said sharply, "Lay off him, Rivers."

I paid no attention to Ivey. "Why, Nick?"

"The lieutenant has given you some good advice," Nick said, and before I could say anything more, Ivey added, "I sure as hell have. Not another peep out of you. Outside, Rivers, and I don't mean ninety seconds from now."

He had signaled the hovering jailer. The cell door was opened. Ivey motioned me out and the jailer crowded me down the corridor between the cells.

I came out on the street under a full head of steam. Okay, fiend, I thought, chalk up another for yourself.

You created this job for me; I didn't want it.

You've put me in deeper than ever. Before this, I needed only enough to build reasonable doubt in the minds of a jury, enough to free Nick. That was my job. That was more than plenty. The police could have had the rest of it, once I'd got enough to free Nick.

Now my job is different. You've made it a lot bigger, and I don't like that. You've taken away what choice I had. You've burned all my bridges behind me and given me only one end result that I'll have to reach, if I'm ever to live with myself in the future.

I'll have to find you, fiend, to learn how and why you can reach out invisibly and make a man lie away the tattered remnants of the wreckage of his life.

In a busy downtown drugstore on Franklin Street, I pushed into a phone booth and called Tillie Rollo.

"Yes?" she said, in her softly modulated voice.

"Ed Rivers. Anything on our friend?"

"Not yet. Have you talked with the man downtown?"

"I just came from there," I said. "They can't identify our friend."

"Did the man ask any questions about me?"

"No," I said. "I'm keeping my end of our bargain."

"And my appreciation," she said. "I'll do what I can for you."

"You'd better do your best, or the man may be asking you a lot of questions."

"I'm not accustomed to receiving threats. . . ."

"And I don't make a practice of handing them out," I said. "I'm merely telling you the facts of life. My back is against a wall and I don't like the feel of it."

"I'll keep you posted," she said, and the line went dead.

I left the drugstore and went to a tavern just off Franklin to grab a bite of lunch.

I was finishing the Cuban sandwich and beer when a midday newscast from the radio behind the bar came cutting at me through the babble of talk and rattle of glasses.

The newscaster elaborated and drew out the gory details. The gist of it was that the police had wrapped up the triple murder which had rocked Tampa. Nick Martin had confessed.

The same voice was bleating from a similar plastic box in Helen Martin's room.

I threw a bill on the bar, slid off the stool, and elbowed my way to the phone booth in front.

I closed the booth, dropped a coin in the slot, and dialed.

The phone at the far end rang.

The little fan inside the booth whirred.

Sweat began squeezing out of my forehead, like brain fluid, under the sudden pressure inside my head.

Again and again her phone was ringing.

Pay phone right outside her door.

House of working people. It was understandable that workdays might often empty the house.

But she'd said she would be there. She wasn't out momentarily, to buy groceries or anything like that. Not at this moment. She'd mentioned that she was catching the newscasts, for what little hope one of them might offer. She wouldn't have missed the important midday newscast.

Her phone kept screaming its fool head off, blindly, purposelessly.

Remembering her discouragement of last night, I had a sickening certainty—her number not only doesn't answer; it's not going to answer.

CHAPTER **12** ▶ ▶ ▶ No MAN is born to be naturally unlucky or lucky. It depends on the turn of mind. If
a man finds solace in thinking of himself as cursed by
continual bad luck, he can prove it to himself by thinking on and magnifying the strokes of tough luck he's
suffered. Subconscious forces will then determine action
and choice favorable to ill luck. The contrary is equally
true of the individual who cannot doubt his luck.

I've always figured that luck, good and bad, just
about evens out.

Right then I was very lucky.

I found a cab, at the hack stand outside the tavern.

It was driven by a co-operative, dark young man of
Latin extraction. When I flashed the photostat of my
license and assured him I would take full responsibility,
he welcomed the diversion from boredom so much his
pencil-thin mustache twitched.

He took me out Florida Avenue with an absolute dis-
regard of traffic laws, life, or property.

He drew rein in front of the old rooming house, the
cab pitching as he locked the brakes. I left a five-dollar
bill in the cab and went into the house.

Up from the gloomy, musty, cooler-than-outside lower
hall.

I caught the first whiffs of the pungent smell when I reached her apartment door.

I opened the door and left it that way. I could hear the pet cocks of the gas stove and space heater hissing.

She'd closed the windows tightly. The sliding portion of the big bay window was stuck. I picked up a chair and smashed it.

Wheeling, I opened a second window, which overlooked the alley at the side of the house.

Another three or four seconds and I had the gas shut off.

Then I turned to Helen. She lay on the old brass bedstead in the small bedroom. One arm dangled from the edge of the bed. The other rested at her side. There was a creeping grayness in her face. Her breathing was shallow and rapid.

I took hold of the head of the bed and swung it so that her face was in the stream of fresh air coming through the smashed window.

There was a small bottle of spirits of ammonia in the bathroom. I used that, plus cold compresses, and chaffed her wrists.

A bubbly moan came from her. I gave her another strong whiff of the ammonia. Her eyes opened. The pupils were dilated, blank. Then they began to focus. She moaned again. A spasm started in her stomach and shook her body.

She murmured something I couldn't understand. I went into the kitchen, covered the bottom of a glass with ammonia and water. I gave her that, a few drops at a time. She was unresisting, as if she didn't realize what she was doing.

Then her faltering functions began to mesh, to operate. She turned on her side, held her head, and gasped, "What a terrific headache!"

"Lie still and gulp that fresh air," I said. "I'll get some coffee going."

I made coffee and looked in the bathroom for aspirin. None was there. On a hunch, I searched the purse in the bedroom. Amid her lipstick, wallet, keys, compact, was a small tin of aspirin. I gave her three of them with steaming black coffee.

Later, she sat on the edge of her bed. Her elbows were on her knees. Her knuckles pressed her temples. The thick, silver-stranded auburn hair fell about her face. A faint touch of color was beginning to stain her cheeks, but she still looked plenty haggard.

"I'm sorry, Ed," she whispered. "If you only knew how sorry I am."

"Sure," I said. "You're okay now."

"How could I have done such a thing? What happened to me in that moment I heard the newscast?"

"Helen . . ."

"No, no, don't try to excuse me. What kind of a creature am I?"

"You're a human being," I said.

"Suddenly I just hated everything, Ed, including myself. The weight of all the years seemed to focus into that one moment and come crashing down on me. I wasn't thinking very much of Nick, was I?"

"No, you weren't."

She sat thinking. She raised her head. "Nick confessed," she cried suddenly. "It's all over for him. How can I go on, Ed?"

"That's the way you were thinking a little while ago," I reminded her bluntly.

Her hand came to her mouth. She bit her knuckles. "That's true! I'm scared, Ed. Scared of myself."

"I don't think you'll try it again, then."

"No, I'm too scared for that." She stood shakily. My

88

impulse was to help her, but I remained standing perfectly still.

"I'll have some more coffee, I believe," she said. She made it to the kitchenette under her own power. Then I helped her into a chair and poured a second cup of coffee for her.

"I'm feeling better now, Ed. You won't call a doctor or anybody, will you?"

"Do want me to?"

"No. A doctor would have to report what happened. I wouldn't want Nick to know."

"Nick will never know," I said.

Tears came to her eyes. She didn't say anything. She reached out and touched my hand.

I stayed with her another two hours. We didn't talk much, and then it was about inconsequential things. During the time, I called a repair shop.

A man came up to fix the broken window before I left. He was a big guy loaded with a lot of belly. Some of the gas smell must have lingered. He sniffed and said, "You got a leaky gas pipe."

"No," I said. "A pot boiled over and put out the flame. It's an old-fashioned stove. Doesn't have a pilot light."

Carrying his tool kit, he followed his stomach into the bedroom. He measured the window and started chipping the old putty.

"How'd it happen?"

"I was swatting at a termite," I told him, "and missed him."

Steve Ivey knew how to be blunt in his refusal.

He stood behind his desk in the quiet of his office. "No," he said, "you cannot see Nick Martin."

"Are you afraid for me to see him?"

89

"No."

"Then why—"

"No."

"Your needle is stuck, Ivey."

"It won't be the only thing stuck if you don't stop trying my patience. Find yourself another case. You've done what you can for your client."

"Life would be simpler if I could think in those terms," I said, facing Ivey across the desk. "But I can't help feeling a greater responsibility toward Nick. The only thing I've done for him is make the eight ball considerably bigger. Before, at least the state's attorney had the job of proving him guilty before a jury. Somebody is afraid, Ivey, feeling the pressure. And Nick is worse off than if I'd never entered the case."

"Any ideas?"

"Plenty. I think Nick did what he did because of Sime Younkers' visit here this morning. I think Sime put the squeeze on Nick, either with a threat against Helen's life or a promise that Helen would be given financial assistance. Nick felt he had to take the offer. It was the only way he could protect Helen or provide for her future. After all, what did he have to lose? So far he's seen no hope of beating this rap. He'd be trading merely the physical wreckage of himself."

"Proof?"

"I can't prove the sun will rise tomorrow, but my reason tells me so. I've had nothing but my reason to show me anything about this case. It was reasonable that an unknown party went to the Yamashita house the day of the murders—there had to be an unknown if Nick didn't kill those people. It was reasonable that the unknown intended to kill only Ichiro, since the parents were expected to be out until after dinner. It was reasonable to believe that the parents had been killed with the motive being to shut them up.

"Now, I know Nick and Helen, Ivey. And I know Sime Younkers. Bearing these factors in mind, what I think about Nick's statement is reasonable."

"And I think," Ivey said, "that Sime wheedled his way to Nick to offer his services and dry-clean, via retainers, the Martins of the little money they have."

"Only one thing wrong with that. If Sime wanted to sell a bill of goods, wouldn't he have chosen Helen Martin as the more likely prospect? She'd grasp at any straw. She'd be more receptive—and she has that little money you spoke of."

"You still can't see Martin," Ivey said, "and that closes the interview. I'm a mole, Rivers, trying to gnaw through a ten-foot concrete wall of work. Martin's statement is a matter of record. Proof. Black-and-white proof. Not the rationalization of a bullheaded man." He picked up a sheaf of papers. "Good day."

It took me until early evening to get a lead on Sime Younkers. I started with his last known address, a cheap hotel. He'd moved downgrade, into rattraps. On his second move, the lead petered out. The seedy old man at the desk of the flophouse was a new employee. He knew nothing about Sime Younkers. The previous desk man had drifted out of town, no one knew where.

I finally located a woman friend of Sime's in an Ybor City beer joint. She had a beer-bloated stomach, pouches under her eyes, and hair like tinder-dry excelsior, showing the remains of three or four shades of old dye.

She knew me, and she knew that I wouldn't be after Sime out of friendship.

She sat across the scarred table from me amid the sour smell of the place and kneaded her knuckles on the table top.

91

She sold Sime out for a five-dollar bill.

She gave me a West Tampa address.

When I left, she was building a new hangover on her old one.

CHAPTER **13** ▶▶▶ THE STREET did not exemplify the best in the American way of life. It was narrow and dark, with trash littering the gutters. Old buildings of brick and wood, scabbed with the dirty remains of old paint, cowered in rows broken by shanties and empty, wood-grown fields.

I parked the rented buggy and took a walk. My heels were loud on the uneven brick paving of the sidewalk. A tired, harassed-looking storekeeper watched me pass from the doorway of his hole in the wall. A few shadowy figures shuffled along the sidewalk. In Ybor City there is at least contrast, famous restaurants around the corner from squalor. In Ybor City there is that undercurrent, that animal zest for the living, like the hot pulsing of Latin blood, that you'll find nowhere else. Here, there was no contrast, no zest.

I checked building numbers, reached the end of the block, and stopped. I stood wiping my face with my handkerchief. The number the woman had given me didn't exist.

I moved back along the sidewalk and, about the middle of the block, I saw the shack. It was a small, boxlike shadow in the lighter shadows of night. Set at the rear of a vacant lot where scraggly palmetto struggled for life against rusty chunks of tin and other junk, the shack was

92

half obscured by the rotting brick building that fronted the sidewalk. Coming down the sidewalk, I'd missed it. From this angle, I saw it.

I turned off the sidewalk. A tangled mass of junk wire caught my ankles and almost tripped me as I crossed the lot.

The shack was dark and silent. It had to be the one. The number no longer remained on the post of the sagging porch. My flicking pencil flashlight revealed the tacks that had once held the tin number. The number would have fitted between the numbers of the buildings fronting the sidewalk on either side of the vacant lot.

I moved up the short wooden steps. The porch creaked under my weight.

The doorknob was loose enough to rattle when I touched it. But it finally caught the catch and the door swung open, hinges complaining softly.

The heat inside the shack was so intense it was a kind of silent crackling. I closed the door and stood a moment.

The surge and roar of life in Tampa might have been on another planet. The only primary indication that anyone had lived in the shack recently was the smell of something rotting in the kitchen.

I played the beam of the pencil flash around. A broken-down wicker set was in this outer room. A threadbare Palm Beach coat, greasy and stiff with grime, lay across the arm of a chair.

I picked the coat up. It was a twin to the one Sime had been wearing when he'd let himself into my office. Or the same coat.

I fished through the pockets. I got no bites. The pocket yielded a lot of tobacco crumbs, a mashed package with a couple of cigarettes in it, and some matchbooks advertising a soft drink.

I dropped the coat on the chair. The shack, I guessed,

93

consisted of three rooms—this one, a kitchen, a bedroom.

A lot of sand had been tracked into the shack. It rasped softly between my shoe soles and the bare planks of the floor.

The door of the bedroom stood open. The pencil flash picked up an old chest of drawers and an iron three-quarter bed. The bed linens consisted of a wrinkled sheet and a lumpy-looking pillow with the impression of somebody's head in it.

I took a couple of steps in the bedroom. My angle of vision widened.

Sime Younkers was lying dead on the floor beyond the bed.

He was sprawled on his side, his under arm sticking out awkwardly behind him. One knee was drawn up a little. His mouth was open, the lips as slick and dry as cellophane, though a dark spot showed where spittle had run out of his mouth onto the floor. His eyes bulged with that glassy glare that comes only from the first glimpse into the bottomless depths of eternity.

He had been struck hard on the back of the head. Gnats were gathering, a small black-swarming cloud over the clotted blood.

I went beside him, shooed the gnats away with a wave of my hand, and tried the pockets of his pants. He owned forty-odd cents in change, a small ring of keys, and a cracked leather wallet.

I examined the wallet and the fishing got better. The wallet contained a crisp new fifty-dollar bill, plus an outdated driver's license, a photostat of his old private-agency license, and four of his old calling cards, little frames of soil around their edges.

On the back of one of the cards, Sime had at some time or other jotted an address.

A Davis Islands address.

94

Victor Cameron's.

I kept the calling card with the address on it and put the rest of Sime Younkers' earthly estate back in his pockets.

I checked the rest of the shack and went outside. As I stepped from the porch I heard the slap of palmetto against a leg.

I started to turn. I never made it. I believe a black-jack was used. It laid itself hard against my skull. My knees knocked together and I pitched on my face.

The pain was like a knife piercing me from ear to ear.

I sensed quick movements. I felt hands grasp me under the armpits. I was being pulled, wrestled, and dragged.

A hinge creaked.

More pulling and dragging.

There was the rasp of sand between a shoe sole and the bare boards of the floor.

The steps moved away from me, decisive, rapid.

I tried to fight my way out of it. The pain was too intolerable. I raised one hand gropingly toward my head before I fainted.

The pain was gone for a passage of time. Then it came creeping back. It brought with it a new factor, a new sensation, a fresh torture. As my senses struggled toward a functioning state, I imagined that I lay helpless on a beach as white as bleached bones. It was blistering to the touch, while a sun that glaringly filled the whole of the Florida sky drew all the grease and life out of my flesh.

I groaned and tried to push away from the heat. The need to clear my head, to move, became a raging demand inside of me.

The heat was wrapping me more tightly. I could hear the voice of it, a continuous, snapping sound.

I rolled onto my back and opened my eyes. It was true— the merciless sun was everywhere. A chip of it came falling

95

toward me, a small flame floating earthward with the glaring light its background.

Then I began to remember. I'd been slugged, dragged into the shack.

Now the shack was on fire.

It was a strangely impersonal thought for the first fraction of a second, like wondering what you'll eat for lunch when you're not hungry.

Then the import of it came to me. The emergency relays and controls sprang into action inside of me. I crabbed around toward the front door as another piece of old paper fell from the ceiling and burned toward me.

The front door was ringed in flame. The flame was rolling across the ceiling, billowing around every wall, threatening to close every avenue of escape in seconds.

I lunged into the kitchen. My eyes were stinging and watering until I couldn't see. My lungs and nostrils felt as if they were filled with acid.

I found a doorknob with my groping fingers. It turned, but the door wouldn't open. The door was latched. I didn't have the strength to smash the door open. I found the latch, a dime-store hook latch, and flipped it.

I fell out of the kitchen into the greasy green of low-growing palmetto. I rested there a moment on my hands and knees, gagging the smoke from my lungs.

In the shack behind me glass went brittle and broke in the heat. Out on the street somebody gave a yell.

I crawled across the palmetto patch, reached the back side of a building, and used a drain pipe to pull myself upright.

I stood in the shadows of the building, a trembling in my knees. I looked across at the shack. Flames from it were leaping two or three stories high now. A citizen might as well call a fire department in Canada for all the good it would do the shack.

On the street, the sounds of excitement got louder. People began to filter across the vacant lot toward the shack to take in the spectacle.

I moved along the back of the building, down the side away from the shack.

I crossed the street and went down the sidewalk. At a point opposite the parked car, I recrossed and got in.

A fresh wave of pain came over me. I sat gripping the steering wheel until it subsided.

The next parking place for the car was in front of Helen Martin's rooming house. I was so woozy I didn't believe I could make it on through the tangle of Tampa to my side of town.

My vision was dancing with black polka dots when I knocked on her door.

She answered quickly. Her face captured a moment of shock as she saw my condition. Then she took my arm.

"You'd better come inside and get something under you besides those shaky pins," she said. She helped me to a chair.

"I'll get a doctor," she said.

"No, I'm not seriously hurt. Mainly, I'm sick to my stomach from reaction. If you'll get that ammonia I used on you today and some cold water for my head . . ."

She was already in action. I sipped the spirits of ammonia and water and felt the fine shock of a cold compress on the back of my head.

"The skin isn't broken," she said. "But you've got a prize-winner of a knot. What did it?"

"Blackjack."

"Who?"

"I don't know."

"Do you— But it's thoughtless of me to ask questions right now. What you need is a comfortable spot for collapsing for a good night's sleep."

97

She didn't have to twist my arm. I know that when a lady and gentleman are forced by circumstances to share the same roof, with only one bedroom available, it's considered proper for the lady to have the bed and the gentleman to arrange himself in another room on a couch or chair.

My consideration right then was for a place I could get prone and yield my muscles to their tiredness.

I let Helen help me into the bedroom. She turned back the covers on the large old bed. Next she kneeled and undid my shoelaces, knowing I'd find it difficult to bend over that far. Then she slipped out of the room and closed the door.

I fought the pull of the bed long enough to peel down to my shorts. I draped my clothes over the chair near the bed and crawled between the sheets.

I lay on my stomach and stretched out.

With that, I died for a few hours.

CHAPTER **14** ▶ ▶ ▶ I woke the next morning to the smell of perking coffee. The bed linens were sodden from my sweat, which was not unusual. I had a dull headache, which was. But it was not as bad as it might have been. Once I was up and going it would wear off. I'd have a sore scalp for a few days, but thinking of that fire I was glad to be able to feel the soreness.

I lay a little longer, thinking of Sime Younkers and the way he'd got himself killed. Sime had been asking for trouble a long time. He'd finally tangled with someone who was not hesitant in dishing it out in large and permanent doses. Someone like the person who could kill and mutilate three people. Someone calmly savage enough to kill without mercy every time danger showed its face.

Today I knew one more thing. A man had been in the shack last night. It had taken a man's strength to drag me inside so the reception could be warmed up. He'd seen me on the street. He'd waited, laid for me as I came out of the shack. Which meant that he knew me. This, of course, took in a large portion of the population of Tampa and vicinity. But it helped to know that he was no wandering vagrant, no stranger. The face of the fiend belonged to someone I knew.

I reminded myself that a man's presence in the shack did not rule out the possibility of the fiend wearing a female face. The man last night could have been acting under orders, out of attachment to a female or for pay. Contrariwise, the man might have been the person for whom I was looking.

It did no good to think that I'd lost a chance last night to wrap up the case. I'd done the best I could. I hadn't underrated the person who, from the moment of Ichiro's killing, had bought safety with further slaughter. I'd reached Sime Younkers as quickly as possible. If one seedy old man had not quit a desk job in a rattrap hotel, the lives of several people might have been different today.

I got out of bed and showered. When I got ready to dress I found that Helen had slipped my clothes out and brushed and pressed them.

When I came out of the bedroom, she heard me and came to the door of the kitchen. She looked pale and tired, but she had a steady grip on herself.

She asked if I'd had a good night's rest and how was I feeling. She wasn't very talkative after that until I was finishing a breakfast of eggs, bacon, toast, and coffee.

She sat across the table from me, sipping a cup of coffee as I ate.

"You've made a new man of me, Helen," I said as I polished off the breakfast.

"I'm afraid the new man is in for some bad news." Her eyes were troubled. "Ed, you were on the newscast a little while ago."

"Ivey's connected me with the fire somehow?"

"I'm afraid it's worse than that. He's got a pickup out on you. The autopsy has been done on Sime, witnesses questioned. It's been a busy night for the Tampa police."

"Did the report say how Ivey tagged me?"

"It seems there is a storekeeper out on that West Tampa street. One of those poor little places that stocks sardines, crackers, canned goods, a few staples. The storekeeper saw you last night."

"A haggard man standing in the doorway of his hole in the wall. I remember."

"You attracted his attention," Helen said. "You were looking for house numbers. He saw you cross the vacant lot toward Sime's shack not long before the fire started. He finally identified you from a copy of the photo taken for your license."

"I see," I said. For a moment I was in Ivey's shoes. I was thinking of the scene in his office late yesterday. I knew how this would look to him. I'd wanted very much to make Sime Younkers say he had forced Nick's confession. Maybe I'd tried too hard with Sime, got too rough—then fired the shack to cover things up.

Helen was looking at me with worry and regret. "Ed, if Nick and I had known that the cost to you—"

"Forget that," I said. "It isn't your fault. When a triple killer used that samurai sword to put Nick on a spot, he involved me personally. The personal involvement, little as I might have wanted it, has progressed by stages until

100

now it's about as personal as an involvement can get."

"Ivey will make this very serious for you, Ed?"

"I'm afraid so, with the storekeeper as a witness. That's concrete evidence—against my tale of a phantom fiend I didn't even see myself who skulked and slugged and tried to fry me.

"Ivey's a good cop because he believes only in what he sees, what circumstances show him. That will solve a lot of cases, most cases.

"But now and then comes a case that makes a mask of circumstances. Reason will show you the truth—reasoning on unseen, though knowable factors, not deductive reasoning on circumstances.

"You have to reach out and believe in this kind of reasoning, even if it makes a lie of appearances. To me, what happened last night will mean one thing. The same appearances will make the case against Nick stronger than ever in Ivey's mind."

"Is there anything at all I can do, Ed?"

"Just sit tight. I wish you'd seen Luisa Shaw around the Yamashita summerhouse, knew something about her."

"The blonde call girl."

"That's the one."

"So far, she seems never to have existed."

"She does—or did—exist. Rachie Cameron glimpsed a woman who might have been her a couple of times. Tillie Rollo saw her and talked to her. Ichiro was very well acquainted with her. This whole thing started when Ichiro kept a tryst with Luisa Shaw."

"I knew so little about the Yamashitas, Ed." The frustrated wish to help was a real pain in her eyes.

"I know," I said.

"I've racked my brain, for details, for anything that might help. Only once did Sadao Yamashita, Ichiro's father, speak of his background or the war."

"Japan's defeat leave the little old man with much bitterness?"

Helen shook her head. "He didn't show it. There was a quiet kindness, a humility, an understanding in the old gentleman. He was born in Japan, the son of a well-to-do Japanese exporter. The family decided to expand the enterprise, and Sadao came to the United States shortly before World War II to set up an import end to the business. The export offices, in Japan, were located in Hiroshima, and the first A-bomb took care of that.

"Sadao weathered the loss of his people, the financial loss, and went ahead to the development of his successful business. Unless he was a very good actor or a hundred-per-cent sham, he carried no resentment against the United States for using the bomb. He knew the truth, that a few power-hungry leaders in Japan had started the war. The bomb was used to stop it. Those who died, died to stop it.

"Maybe the nature of his business raised his outlook above artificial national boundaries. He seemed to have a genuine regret for the loss of American boys, as well as Japanese. They were all losses, he said, of the one suffering family of humanity."

"I'll try to remember the loss of that little old man when the time comes," I said. I stood up. "Thanks for everything."

"Be careful, Ed."

"Don't worry on that score. I'd rather be called cautious than corpse. I'll be in touch by phone when necessary. If you don't hear from me right away, don't worry. Ivey'll get around to a routine contact with you. Don't get yourself in trouble. Tell him I came here looking bushed, was a guest for the night, and skipped out before you heard I was the object of a manhunt. Right about now Ivey will be checking my office, the apartment, usual haunts."

If Helen's story to Ivey were to hold, I'd have to get

out of the rooming house without being noticed, without his being able to prove what time I'd left this morning.

I paused in the lower hall. About me, the house was very quiet. I guessed the tenants had all gone to work. Outside was the normal car and pedestrian traffic. The best way to get out of the house without being noticed was to do nothing that would cause notice.

Just another human being, I calmly walked outside, got in the car, and drove away.

I knew that Ivey's organized effort to find me would be most intense during the next forty-eight hours or so. After that, society itself would cause the pressure to taper off. As Ivey had said, murders, muggings, and mayhem didn't cease just because he wanted to track down one man.

I disliked the waste of time, but I knew it would be smart not to gamble a greater waste. Also, I needed a chance to get over the treatment my body had taken during the last five days. Couple the emotional strain with a beating, a slugging, and a scorching, and you find a little tremor under the soreness of the muscles, and tiny naked spots on the nerve ends.

Time, I decided, would be ticking out an efficient job for me. That other man, the handy man with the black-jack, would have to sweat out knowing that I hadn't died in the fire. I was still loose, neither maimed nor detained by the police, looking for him.

I needed a temporary lair, a safe den. I drove crosstown toward Ybor City. I've never picked on the little people over there; on occasion I've done a thing or two for a few of them. I did it with no thought of charity, merely because I couldn't duck the fact that I was able to do it. I did it without expecting return, and I've found gradually that they attach a peculiar importance to that.

I stopped the car in the heart of Ybor City, among the

little people. I mentioned my need with the fewest
necessary words.

Ivey was licked right then in his immediate hunt for
me.

I vanished.

CHAPTER **15** ▶▶▶ By MONDAY afternoon, other
news had crowded me right out of the papers. I shed no
tears over that. They'd had their fun, rehashing events from
a triple murder to the killing of an ex-private detective and
the burning of his body almost beyond recognition, this
latter event apparently being the work of a second private
detective who was trying to spring a client charged with
the triple slaying.

During the weekend I had to buy fresh clothes. I knew
the apartment would be staked out. Feeling much better,
at least in the physical sense, I thanked the family that
had given me protection and a rest cure for the weekend,
and came out on the teeming street just before sundown.

At a corner beanery I was eating *garbanzo* soup with
cold beer on the side, when I learned that Prince Kuriacha
had connections of his own in Ybor City. The affluent
former heavyweight king of wrestlers had dropped the
word that he wanted to see me.

His address reached me via the waiter who brought
deep-fried grouper and a spicy Cuban slaw to follow the
soup.

The Prince was staying at a plush hotel downtown. I
called him from a drugstore phone booth.

His room phone rang about four times. It seemed he

was out, probably at dinner. Then the phone clicked and the natty, hairless gorilla rasped a hello.

"I hear you want to see me," I said.

"Maybe."

"A fellow in Ybor City told me. You know who this is, of course."

"Sure, I know."

"What do you have? I assume it's about the Yamashitas."

"That's right."

A frown creased itself between my eyes. He sounded hesitant, cautious.

"Kuriacha, are you alone?"

He was silent a moment. Then, "Been a long time, all right. Glad you called."

"Okay," I said, "so you can't spill it over the phone."

"That's right. Sure like to see you, talk over old times. Where are you stopping off?"

"No abode at the moment," I said. "Are you in any danger from whoever is there?"

"Hah!" It was an indication that he could take care of himself. "Where are you?"

"I'll call you later," I said.

While I was in the phone booth, I got rid of my immediate calling by ringing Helen Martin and then Tillie Rollo. Nothing new at either spot. Helen was holding up. Tillie had uncovered no trace of Luisa Shaw.

"Relax," I told Tillie. "You sound like you've built a brittle nervous edge."

"And why not? After all, you're a wanted man. I don't want any more truck with this thing."

"We made a bargain," I reminded her.

"Before this thing kept ballooning to such proportions."

"You find Luisa Shaw," I said, "and we'll prick that balloon. You'll still be able to preside over that ultra-exclusive social set in some little town with its single country club."

"Ed—"

"I wouldn't hurry up plans about trying to find that town, if I were you, until matters are settled here."

"Are you threatening me?"

"If you want to put it that way. Luisa Shaw is the key to this thing, Tillie, and I'll take some pretty strong measures to find her."

"I wish I'd never seen the slimy little slut!" Tillie decided as she broke the connection.

The street lights had been turned on when I came out of the drugstore. There was a soft, smothering quality in the early darkness. The air was dead. The bricks, wood, and paving of Ybor City emanated heat like the giant element of an old stove.

Now that I was outside, the best way to move would be quietly and not furtively. Deny the pressure inside. Steer away from the knowledge that Ivey's organization would net me sooner or later. Crouch down behind my eyes and do whatever could be done in whatever time I had left.

The rented car was in a shacky garage behind an old stucco rooming house. Let the Tampa cops wear out their eyeballs looking for it. I didn't go near it. Instead, I borrowed a heap from the owner of a small beer tavern. A rotund little man I'd known for years, he expressed concern about the police in his garbled Spanish-English.

"You don't know the car is gone," I said. "But don't report it stolen right away quick."

A Latin light came to his eyes, compounded of love of conspiracy and adventure.

"You *un* great—how-you-say-in-*inglés*—thinker, Ed. You do me *mucho* favors, past times. Keys on *mesa*. My back I turn to you."

I picked up the keys from the cluttered table he used for a desk. Then I left the small back-room office.

I threaded through the lights and traffic in downtown Tampa, crossed the river, and took the link to Davis Islands.

I parked the buggy on the palm-lined street, and walked up the driveway to the Cameron house.

From the shadows of the shrubs, I watched the house for a while. The living-room windows framed light downstairs. The remainder of the house was dark. From time to time I saw Victor Cameron cross the window. Each time he had a glass in his hand. No sound came from the house. He wasn't watching television, reading, or listening to a hi-fi or radio. He was prowling like a creature whose torment would not permit it to remain still. Drinking, but unable to get drunk.

I scouted the house to make doubly sure he was alone. The rear was dark. The surface of the pool where I'd first met Rachie lay like a sheet of dark-blue, unwrinkled plastic.

At the front of the house once more, I eased onto the veranda. I palmed the knob of the front door and found the door unlocked.

The door opened without noise, and the carpet of the entry foyer deadened my footsteps.

I was just inside the living room before he realized he was not alone any longer. He poured a drink from a cut-glass decanter, turned, saw me, and stood absolutely still for a moment.

"Sorry to break in," I said, "but I didn't want to risk your slamming the door and reaching a telephone."

"What do you want?" He tried to get a little of his old-time bluster and command in his tone.

The lighting from a lamp behind him hollowed his face and heightened the gray, tired look of him.

107

I took Sime Younkers' dirt-ringed calling card from my pocket and dropped it on the table beside the whisky decanter.

He refused to look at the card. He had still not voluntarily moved a muscle, but a tiny one was quivering in the side of his thick neck.

"Turn it over," I said.

"Why should I?"

"Because something is written on the back."

"I'm not at all interested, Rivers."

"You'd better be," I said.

"Indeed? Why?"

"Because I'm giving you a chance—to convince me that you had nothing to do with Sime Younkers' death."

"You're presuming too much. I don't care to take the trouble to talk to you."

I slapped him across the side of his face with my open hand.

He stood rocking. Not from the force or physical pain of the blow. The quivering crawled from the small area on his neck to the corners of his mouth. The gray mists gathered in greater quantity in his eyes. He bit his lip and suddenly ducked his head, to hide from me, to hide from the knowledge that I was seeking. I thought of a small boy who's been kicked out of the club after the most terrible discovery of his life has been made—that he's all bravado.

"You had no reason to do that," he said in a soft, husky voice. "A few years ago I'd have smashed you with my bare hands for such an insult."

"Fears can overpower insults, can't they?"

"I'm not really afraid of you, Rivers. Not physically."

"I'll give you every benefit of that doubt. You're a snob whose snobbery has been undermined. It's left you with nothing. Now if you won't pick up that calling card, I'll tell you about it. It came from the pocket of a dead man. His name was Sime Younkers."

"The only thing I know about him is what I've read in the papers the last couple of days, Rivers."

"The back of the card calls you a liar," I said. "Your address is on it."

"Perhaps you put it there."

"Don't be asinine! In my present spot, would I take a chance on coming out here if I wasn't convinced there was a real connection between you and a man now dead, a man involved in the Yamashita business?"

"You're trying to frame me." He sought to bluster. He raised the glass and tossed off the drink. I sensed the fight inside of him, his seething frustration as he tried to fan new life in the top-heavy ego that had carried him through many years.

I put my hands on my hips and stood looking at him a moment. I had a cankerous frustration of my own.

"I wish you wouldn't be so difficult, Cameron."

"I really don't care to see any more of you." He poured himself another drink. "You'd better leave now."

I took a step toward him. I knew that a man of his disposition would have a particular horror of cold steel. I didn't want to do it. But I reached to the nape of my neck and slid the knife from its sheath.

Lamplight glittered on the blade and etched the edge with almost luminosity.

"You—you wouldn't dare!" Cameron said.

He looked from the blade to my face. The glass slipped from his hand and liquor stained the carpet. The gray of his cheeks faded to dead white. His mouth opened to catch a quick breath.

"You savage!" he whispered.

"I do what has to be done, Cameron. I'm trying to save the life of a man, the future and sanity of his wife, as well

109

as my own skin. If it means coming in your lovely home and scraping the whitewash off you, that's just too damned bad. I'm not going to ask you again. What business did you have with Sime Younkers?"

Cameron backed from the knife until the table touched him below his hips. "I—retained him. On a matter that had nothing to do with the Yamashitas or Younkers' death."

"What was it?"

"A personal thing. I told you. Nothing came of it."

"I like to know personal things," I said.

Unconsciously, he beat the meaty edge of his palm against the edge of the table. "I thought Sadao's son, Ichiro, was stealing from the firm."

"You hired Sime Younkers to find out?"

"Yes."

"What did he find?"

"I was wrong. Ichiro was innocent."

"What caused you to suspect him in the first place?"

"The way he lived. The cost of it."

"I checked Ichiro's financial affairs myself, Cameron. You'd better think of something else. Everything was in order."

A thing drew tight inside of him and snapped. He stopped striking the edge of the table. "I don't care what you checked! Ichiro was living high. I had reasons for my suspicions. Sime Younkers had a license then, and my action was perfectly legitimate. Certainly you found Ichiro's affairs in order. He'd spent beyond his means, but someone had let him have some money."

I studied his face carefully. "Rachie?"

"If you must know, yes. Now all the skeletons are out in the open."

"Rachie get the money from you?"

"Money doesn't mean much to Rachie. Rachie's mother was not exactly a pauper when she died."

"Ichiro pay Rachie back?"

Cameron stared at me. "Smart as you think you are, Rivers," he said bitterly, "you're built on the bedrock of naïve puritanism."

"So I've been told. Thanks. Now I dig you."

"I wonder if you do really?" he said in a hollow voice. He blundered toward a chair and sat down, his hands dangling limp over the arms of the chair.

"She got a charge out of buying him," Cameron said in that same voice, "the same way some pathologically cruel people enjoy buying an animal."

He sat gazing haggardly at the carpet, perhaps seeing her face as it had been years ago, when the misty sweetness of childhood hid the thing waiting to grow inside of her.

"Did you go to the Yamashita summerhouse the day they were killed, Cameron?"

"No," he said, without turning his head.

"Did Rachie?"

"I don't know," he said dully. A short, bitter laugh ripped out of him. "The whole truth, Rivers, that's what I'm telling now. I honestly don't know if she went out there. Even if she did, it would have been with Ichiro. She'd have no reason to kill the whole family."

"There was another woman out there," I said.

He looked up. His eyes came into focus. "Another woman?"

"Her name is—or was—Luisa Shaw. Pert, blonde, very good looking. Do you know her?"

"I—no."

"Your hesitation is showing."

"I've heard the name."

"When?"

"About a week before the murders."

"Where?"

"Here," Cameron said bleakly, "in my own house. Ichiro and Rachie came in. They didn't know I was home, could overhear. She was asking him about Luisa Shaw. She—made a comparison between herself and Luisa."

"Do you know what Luisa is?"

Cameron peered at images hidden in the carpet again. "Yes."

"Did Rachie sound jealous of Luisa Shaw in her talk with Ichiro that day?"

"No. She sounded as if she were getting a kick out of talking about herself and Luisa to the man who knew them both."

"She might have developed a jealousy," I said. "She might have been hiding it that day."

"I don't know."

"She might have gone out to the Yamashita house when Luisa and Ichiro were there," I said. "She might have flown into an insane rage."

"And—killed them?"

"Ichiro, then the parents when they arrived before she could get away."

Short, crazy dribbles of laughter, increasing in tempo, came from Cameron's lips. "Rachie do that?"

"Rachie do that," I echoed.

The laughter went out of him. He wiped his hand across his lips. He glanced toward the table. He was already saturated with whisky, but he got up and gulped another drink.

"You just don't know her, Rivers," he said, pouring another slug. "Rachie might even find an insane pleasure in the glimpse of blood, but she'd never risk her own skin. That's one thing about these people called beat. Their own dainty hides and unweaned egos have become so precious they cannot be exposed to the slightest of the world's thorns. Nothing must mar the preciousness. Nothing else

112

matters except the preciousness, even if it must hide in fantasy or oblivion."

He threw the fresh drink down his throat. "Rivers," he snarled suddenly, "I'm beginning to get drunk, good and stinking drunk. Why the hell don't you leave me alone? You and your damned knife. So I didn't like it. I've never liked it. I never will like the thought of a knife. You've made me spit her out before you. My daughter. Now why don't you get out of here? Haven't I had plenty on my back?"

"Yes," I said, "I guess you have."

"Damn right I have. My friends killed. All the details of the aftermath falling on me. Not just a funeral. Oh, no. I got to make all the arrangements for three of them. All at once. You ever do a grim job like that, Rivers?"

"I've been spared that kind of ordeal," I said.

He picked up decanter and glass and poured another three ounces of whisky into his suffering blood stream.

He gagged a little on it this time. For a second his eyes crossed.

He fumbled for the table top to hold himself. "But I'll bet you could do it, Rivers. Bury three people—never turn a hair—you damned savage . . ."

I'd figured to lock him in a closet when I left to keep him from phoning the police too quickly about my visit. I was spared the trouble.

His elbow collapsed. The hand on the table top, supporting him, slipped. He staggered against the table. It turned over. The expensive whisky ran out on the carpet.

I caught Cameron to keep him from falling. I helped him toward a candy-striped divan and laid him down. He made a soft, meaningless mumble in his throat. His eyes were closed. The mumble stopped.

He passed out. His shallow, rapid breathing made small spit bubbles at the corner of his loose mouth.

113

CHAPTER **16** ▶ ▶ ▶ Rachie Cameron had entered the house the same way I had. Silently.

As I turned from Cameron, I stopped moving. Rachie was framed in the living-room archway. She was cool and lovely in white linen. Her short black hair was mussed as if she'd been riding in an open car.

"Greetings, ugly man."

"Where's the boy friend?"

"I haven't had one handy," she said, answering the question in my mind as to whether or not she was alone. "Except you."

She took a few careless steps toward me. She was carrying a small handbag. She tossed it on a chair, raised her arms, stretched. "I'm not mad at you any longer, ugly man."

"That's good," I said. "But since my age and constitution were questionable the last time we met, I could remind you that I'm a little older."

"Not much." She looked at her father, wrinkled her nose. "He smells. Let's go back to the playroom and have a drink."

"Sorry," I said.

She tilted her head. "Why are you so hard to get acquainted?"

"I'm not," I said. "Just working."

"And look what all that work has got you. Swarms of policemen on the lookout for you."

"Then you can see how limited my time is," I said.

She stood quite close to me. Her lazy eyes searched the crevices and lumps of my face. "Will you kill if they corner you?"

"Don't be ridiculous!"

"They don't have to corner you at all," she said. "You could go away."

"I forgot to buy a plane ticket."

"Why bother with noisy airports. I've got a perfectly lovely car."

Her arms slipped about my neck. I reached up and gripped her wrists.

"Honey," I said, "I think I'd be safer taking my chances with all those armed cops."

"Now you're being mean to me again!" Her voice was petulant. She couldn't stand being denied anything. I expected her to stamp her foot in undisciplined, unbridled rage.

"Too bad some of the young swains of this town haven't learned the combination long ago," I said.

"What combination?"

"Skip it," I said.

She stood on tiptoe. "Afraid to kiss me?"

"I'm afraid of everything about you."

I jerked her arms loose.

"Oh, you damned beast!" she seethed, rubbing her wrists. Without warning, she turned suddenly and ran. I lunged after her.

She darted into the hallway, down it to a door. The slammed door almost broke my nose. She was as quick as agitated mercury, throwing the bolt inside.

I put my shoulder against the door. It held. She was

115

very quiet in the room. Then, my ear against the door, I heard a clicking. The clicking of a telephone dial. Her muffled voice: "Operator, this is an emergency. Get me the police."

For a second, the way I felt toward Rachie Cameron made me as cold as a dead man.

Like any islands, Davis Islands are surrounded by water. A simple matter to seal it off. Steve Ivey himself couldn't have arranged a better setup for trapping me.

I took a step back from the door and made a pile driver of my leg. My heel struck the door at the lock. Wood splintered and metal twanged. The door was a flashing movement on its hinges. It crashed against the wall.

Rachie jerked around. "Davis Islands, operator," she yelped. "Cameron residence—"

She tried to duck past me. I grabbed a handful of the linen dress. With the other hand I caught the phone cord and tore it out by the roots.

She fought like a savage little animal that should be caged in a pigsty, clawing, kicking, spewing shocking words from her sweet-looking face.

I heard the shoulder of the linen dress rip. I didn't have time to be courteous. I picked her up bodily and threw her into the closet, turned the latch.

Filled with the dead heat as it was, the night air outside felt good on my face. Behind me, the house appeared serene. A rubber-necking tourist passing the estate might have envied the occupants.

As I neared the short bridge to the mainland, a police car, red light blinking, swung off the mainland boulevard. It came across the bridge fast, and like any good motorist, I pulled over and stopped until the police car was past.

I slipped back into Ybor City, parked the car in an alley, and used the rear door to the small office of the beer tavern.

116

The round-faced, ever-cheerful owner was at his cluttered desk-table working laboriously on some bills.

"'Ay-lo, Ed. The car vamoose okay?"

"Fine," I said. I dropped the keys on the desk.

"Keep," he said, "I use car ver' leetle. 'Ave next set."

He took a spare set of keys out of the table drawer to show me his "next" set.

"You'll be paid for use of the car," I said.

"Okay. I know. You wailcome to car, but *dinero* nice to get. I know you pay. You know, *hombre* in Ybor City looking for you."

"Who?"

"Beeg beembo. How you say—Keeng?" He made violent motions with his hands, got a headlock on an imaginary foe, and threw him.

"Prince?" I suggested. "Prince Kuriacha?"

"You so right," he said, a pleased smile wreathing his face.

"Where is he now?"

A shrug of the round, plump shoulders.

"Do you know what he wanted?"

"No. Ees serious?"

"Could be."

"Nobody tell. Nobody see you."

"Thanks."

"He ver' famous man. No come in my place bayfore. I see him in reeng two, thray time. *Mucho* time ago. He say he send beeg *fotografía* weeth his name sign. I hang eet over bar. Haylp bees-ness."

"You'll have to order beer by the tanker load."

He grinned warmly, shyly. "My leg, eet's being pulled."

The sudden move on Kuriacha's part made me want to see him as badly as he seemed to want to see me. I went out looking for him. If he was still in Ybor City that night,

117

we kept missing each other, like people trying to catch up with each other in a revolving door.

Nobody could tell me very much about him that I didn't already know. Kuriacha was not his real name, though he had used it so many years it had become real enough by adoption. He'd mentioned to me once that California was his background. He'd started wrestling out there and moved into the big time before he ever came East. The cross-breeding that has taken place in certain areas of the West Coast was what gave the Prince his decidedly Oriental appearance.

It was very late when I tried phoning Kuriacha's hotel. His room did not answer.

I took my tired feet up the steps of a cheap hotel and got a room. While I could trust the desk clerk, it was not as safe as the home that had sheltered me for the weekend.

I locked the door and put the .38 handy on the rickety bedside table. While I was undressing, I sipped away at a pint can of cold beer I'd brought in with me.

Later, lying on the lumpy bed that creaked a protest every time I flickered a muscle, I watched the winking glow of a neon sign across the street. On and off. Off and on. Senseless, mindless. Like the slaughter of three people on Caloosa Point.

I was plenty long in thought right then. The dirty little room seemed to have a loneliness all its own.

I thought of Nick and Helen, of the poor devil on Davis Islands and his daughter, of what Sime Younkers might have told me if I'd reached him sooner.

I wondered what the home office was thinking about me and when they would send a man down.

I realized I was on the point of feeling sorry for myself, and I forced a little laugh at Ed Rivers. Pretty grim, but still a laugh.

I knew a lot more now than when I'd started. I'd

118

recognized the how in the case when I'd eliminated the elder Yamashitas from the motive. I still lacked that stuff Steve Ivey called concrete evidence, but I was more certain than ever that Ichiro's death had been the primary aim, everything else a murderously logical aftermath.

So much for the how and wherefore.

Off and on went the neon light, a silent measure of time as my thoughts clicked away. I balanced every word, action, fact.

And suddenly a prickling sensation flew all over me.

I could almost glimpse the who. I suspected, but I couldn't be sure.

I wouldn't be sure until I had found Luisa Shaw.

CHAPTER **17** ▶▶▶ I FOUND myself back in the newspapers the next morning.

Disheveled, delectable morsel in a torn dress, Rachie Cameron had fallen in the arms of the cops who'd found her, with the wild tale that I'd come out to Davis Islands and tried to assault her. Her father must have been much drunker much earlier than I'd thought, in one of those sober-appearing, straight-walking stages certain individuals can get in with a part of the brain literally paralyzed. He claimed he didn't remember much of what happened.

The story had all the elements. The Cameron name. Sweet young thing innocently walking into her own home to find a big monster, already wanted by the police, lurking on the premises. Steve Ivey was quoted as saying that efforts to find me would be redoubled. Which meant he'd

119

break another brain cell trying to figure where he could pull some men to put back on my trail.

It might have been a delightful break in boredom for Rachie, a thrill with both masochistic and sadistic elements mixed in, a source of satisfaction to know how much trouble she could cause me—but it was hell for me. Much more of this, and I wouldn't have a friend anywhere, even in Ybor City.

Right then, I could have gladly jerked her bald, smashed her over my knee, and whipped her with the bloody scalp until nothing was left of it.

Instead, I wondered how safe the hotel room was going to remain.

I had no choice but to wait and find out. I knew the dangers of being on open streets in broad daylight right now. The hotel room was by far the best prospect.

Without breakfast, I prowled the room, people-watched from the window, read, down to the classified ads, the paper I'd bought on the corner that morning before I'd known my picture would look back at me from the front page and send me back to the room fast.

By early afternoon, I began to relax. If no longer clammed up tight, Ybor City had volunteered no information, or Ivey's men had asked the wrong people.

From the hall phone I called a beanery and had some grub sent up. While I was waiting, I tried Kuriacha's hotel. His room failed to respond.

I got my coin back and slugged the phone again with it, calling Helen Martin. I assured her I was still in one piece and trying.

The next call was to Tillie Rollo.

There was a lengthy silence at her end after we exchanged hellos.

"Where are you, Ed?" she asked tightly.

"Never mind that. You know why I'm calling."

"Of course."

The phone hummed through a silence of my own. "Is someone else there?"

"No!" she said quickly.

"You sound upset."

"Naturally. I read the papers this morning. There's nothing for you at this end."

"No?"

"The person has left town."

"What makes you so sure."

"I—I'd have heard," she said.

"Maybe not."

"Yes, I would have. I've inquired and looked. It's no good. Please leave me alone. I can't help you."

Click.

I put the phone on its hook and went back to the room to take care of the tray of food a dark-skinned boy brought up.

Hungry as I was, I didn't think much about the food, eating without really tasting it. My mind was too much on Tillie Rollo.

As soon as I had eaten, I returned to the hall pay phone. I got Helen Martin on the line.

"I want you to do me a favor," I said.

"Anything I can, Ed."

"Call the airports and train station. Tell them your name is Miss Rollo and say you want to ask about your reservation."

"Will do."

I gave her the number of the pay phone. "Then call me back."

"Right away."

A ten-minute wait. The phone jangled.

"Ed?" Helen asked.

"Yes."

121

"I did as you asked. They didn't know anything about a reservation."

"It means she hasn't got one," I said, "and that's what I wanted to know. You want to stick your neck out a little?"

"If it would help you and Nick I'd be grateful for the chance."

"I'm pinned down for the moment, but I've got to make sure a pigeon doesn't leave the nest."

"Just tell me what to do."

I gave her Tillie Rollo's address. "Drive out there and park where you can see the house, but not too close. The madam is a very chic redhead. Never mind that too much. Just keep an eye on the place. She drives a foreign-built sport car. If a woman, or the car, leaves the house, call me immediately."

"I'm on my way, Ed."

"One more thing, and don't you forget this. Pick your spot carefully. There's a small, elite shopping center about a block or so away. It would be ideal. I want the house watched, but I don't want the house to know it. If anyone approaches you, man or woman, leave and call me. Don't dare take a single chance."

"I won't, Ed."

"I'll see you later."

Later was shortly after dark. I pulled the borrowed heap in behind the old but clean car that belonged to the Martins.

The buildings of the small shopping center gleamed like pearl in the glow of street lamps. The center had closed for the night, except for the drugstore.

I got out of the borrowed car and walked toward Helen's. She was near the corner of the parking area, inconspicuous among the three or four cars belonging to patrons of the drugstore.

The Rollo house, an isolated, snug miniature estate, was

not fully visible from this point, but the view was a clear shot of the long, wide, straight street.

Helen leaned her head a little out of the window and looked up to talk to me as I stopped beside her.

"Anything doing?"

"It's been perfectly quiet down there," she said. "Not a soul left or entered, unless it was by the back way."

"Good."

"Ed . . ." Hope, and the fear of hoping, mingled in her strained face. "You've got something important, haven't you?"

I hesitated. Then I told her, "We've been taking a clobbering against the ropes. After I talk to Tillie Rollo we may be able to start punching our way out of it."

She couldn't help the sudden tears any more than she could stop breathing.

"Easy," I said.

She managed a smile. "Don't you know we foolish women have to get misty sometimes from a good thing as well as a bad?"

I started to caution her, to remind her that Tillie hadn't opened up yet, that I could be wrong, that we were still in about as deep a hole as mortals can get into.

I didn't say it. At this stage, what good would it do to deny her a ghost of hope?

Her fingers were gripping the car window molding. I gave her hand a squeeze.

"You've done your stint, Helen. Now I want you to get out of the neighborhood."

She nodded and started the car. I waited until she had reached the street and turned the corner.

I parked the borrowed chariot about a hundred yards from Tillie's place and walked to the elegant little cesspool.

The house was softly lighted. The sport car glinted in

123

the half light like a crouching black leopard under the carport.

I didn't ring. Now that I was here, I moved quickly across the manicured lawn, skirting shrubs, and paused in the carport.

I tried the door providing side entry into the house from the carport. The door was unlocked, and I let myself in.

I passed through a gleaming kitchen, the dining room. At the edge of the living room, I stopped. There was no sign of Tillie and the house was perfectly silent.

Then I heard a faint sound that seemed to come from the hallway off the living room.

I crossed the living room and entered the hall. There was light in the hall, coming from an open doorway a few feet away.

I reached the doorway, and there was Tillie in her bedroom, moving from closet to wardrobe trunk, which stood open beside the silken-covered bed.

Tillie was coolly and properly lovely in a black, light-weight suit. She arranged a couple of dresses in the wardrobe trunk.

As she started to rise, she glanced in the huge, perfect mirror of the dressing table. She stopped breathing for a second, and we examined each other in the mirror. She watched as the bearish, slope-shouldered figure in the mirror came out of the background.

In the mirror I watched the quick flow of expression on her face. Near panic, briefly. Then anger. Then a hood dropping over the green eyes. The hood was invisible, of course. But you knew it was there. You had to look through it to see the eyes, and it did something to them.

"There wasn't a telephone handy," I said.

"That's too bad. You could have saved yourself a trip out here." She turned to the dressing table, picked up a

124

package of cigarettes, and lighted one to steady herself.

"I didn't mind the trip, Tillie. I figured you'd rather put me straight on Luisa Shaw in person."

"I don't know what you're talking about."

"Same thing we've been talking about, honey."

"Really, you've been stretching things because of your desperation. I don't know Luisa Shaw, never saw her but that one time. I suspect she's far away from Tampa by this time, and I don't really care. There's nothing I can do for you, Ed, and I think you'd better leave now."

"So you can finish your packing?"

"That's right."

"Going to hunt that faraway little town sooner than you expected?"

"I believe that's my business." Her voice was steady, but there was a pinched whiteness showing through the make-up on her clear, lovely face.

"You weren't thinking of leaving a few days ago."

"Wasn't I?"

"You didn't say anything about it."

"That proves something?"

"You were willing to try to help me find Luisa Shaw so you could be protected and stay here. I believe that's the way it was."

"You seem to have drawn some wrong impressions, Ed."

"Such as the impression that since I was out here the other day somebody has scared the hell out of you?"

There was a momentary spoilage of her poise and lady-like demeanor in the quick, hard way she dragged at the cigarette. "Why would anyone do that?"

"Because I'm trying to find Luisa Shaw and you might be a way."

"I don't discuss my business with every sloppy-looking bear who barges in here, Ed, which is why I said nothing to you of my plans the other day. I've done as I promised.

125

I inquired after Luisa Shaw for you. Don't you appreciate that?"

"I'd appreciate it a lot more if you'd tell me who doesn't want me to find her."

"Okay," she said, "I'll tell."

I waited. "Who?"

"A figment of your imagination. But I'll tell you one thing. This Shaw business only solidified my plans to leave. It's shown me that as carefully and rigidly as I conduct my business, I can't stay out of the records forever, what with people like you around. It's proven to me that one day one of my girls will do something foolish and I'll be dragged in. After all, I have enough now, with my stocks, bonds, savings, and the price this house will bring."

"A woman like you never has enough, Tillie. I'll put you wise to yourself. For years you've kidded yourself. You've set a goal that helps you kid yourself. Actually, you like what you're doing. You like the money and the ease and your power over the girls."

Hatred was sudden and naked in her eyes. Then the hood washed over the green depths again. "You're wrong about my not wanting the respectability, the husband, the place in society, Ed. I do like power. I like the power I have now. But it's nothing compared to the power I want, the power I'll have."

"Suit yourself," I said, "and leave now to search out your nameless little town and respectable husband. I won't delay you another five seconds. All I want is a name—or Luisa Shaw's address."

"I don't know either. . . ."

I caught the collar of her jacket the way I would a man's. I snapped her around and opened my mouth to speak as the shot came from outside, punched a neat hole in the window and a messy one in Tillie's neck. The bullet entered the back of her neck, struck bone, was

126

deflected, and angled up and out. It nipped by my shoulder and I heard it strike the wall behind me, its power spent, and fall to the floor.

A red gusher poured from the side of Tillie's neck. I felt a paralysis grip her entire body. Her head fell over to rest on her shoulder.

She looked at me with eyes that pleaded desperately for life.

I knocked the lamp from the dressing table and fell with Tillie to the floor. In the darkness I heard the tortured hiss of breath, in and out, through torn flesh.

He hadn't meant to kill her. He'd set a trap, thrown an intense scare into her, baiting the trap with that fear. He'd known that it would prod me into coming here. Unwittingly, Tillie had been manipulated. Unwillingly, she'd saved my life.

CHAPTER **18** ▶▶▶ YOU'RE IN your living room one evening and you hear a distant, sharp sound in the night. You glance at your wife or husband. Maybe you even get up and turn down the TV.

"Sounded like a shot," you say. Could have been a car backfire. You listen a moment and if you hear nothing else you end up feeding the volume again on the television set.

So it was the night of Tillie's death. If anyone heard the shot, it was not with sufficient alarm to cause a call to the police.

We were left alone, me and the man outside. I got out of the house by the simple process of crawling through

127

the dark hallway to the glass-enclosed Florida room, across the play area to the open patio.

Nervous tremors ran through my knees and quickened my hands. I had the .38 ready as I reached the corner of the house.

I saw no sign of him, only the shadows of trimmed shrubs. Keeping low and close to the house, I moved forward. Nothing else stirred in the dead, hot darkness. If he was laying for me, it was with a care and coolness that made me hate to think of the outcome.

I inched from shrub to shrub. I crossed the spot where he must have worked his way to get a clear shot through the window.

Then, from down the street, I heard a car start quietly and move away.

Tillie Rollo was dying. No one could live long with a hole like that in the neck. So I gambled that the man in the car was the right man, and I finished a circuit of the house more boldly.

The sigh-sob bubbling of Tillie's breath was still audible when I returned to her bedroom.

The lamp was broken from its fall to the floor. I pulled the pencil flashlight from my pocket and put the small beam on her face.

Her skin was slick with sweat. Her teeth gleamed behind her parted lips. Her eyes were fever hot.

"Tillie, can you hear me?"

She lay looking at faraway sights only she could see, smiling her ghastly smile.

"Tillie, if you can still speak—"

"How are you?" she said, in a gurgling whisper.

"Tillie—"

"It was nice of you to come. It's only a little party, really, but I thought I'd better engage the country club. You know everyone, I'm sure. Do have a drink."

She couldn't move a muscle, and yet she glided about an imaginary country club in an imaginary little town.

"Oh, hello there. How was Bermuda? We're planning a short jaunt this winter. It's wonderful having you back. . . ."

She cautioned the caterer and gave instructions to the orchestra.

The imaginary music started.

She was laughter. She was graciousness and beauty as she danced. She mingled and added that special spark that made the affair an event, not just a party. The society section of tomorrow morning's newspaper would be topped by a glowing description of the scintillating gathering.

The dream was real for Tillie at last. She had just enough time for the last guest to depart, leaving the queen of society tired but satisfied. Enough time for the rich, indulgent husband to put his arm around her waist and tell her that she was wonderful, darling.

Then Tillie died.

With the pencil flashlight, I looked for the slug that had killed her. I found it at the base of the hardwood-paneled wall. Wrapping it in my handkerchief, I dropped it in my pocket.

I chose the back way out of the house. I'd already made plenty of footprints in the soft greenery of the yard. A few more wouldn't matter.

I returned to the borrowed heap and drove toward downtown Tampa, where the lights made a diffused pink halo in the night sky.

I kept myself from thinking that another link to Luisa Shaw had been cut. I wouldn't dwell on the fact that the other man, by sheer ruthlessness and lack of mercy, had stayed one jump ahead of me all the way.

I crossed the river, turned off the boulevard, and drove

129

down the wide, palm-lined street. I didn't stop for a considerable distance. Then I turned the car around in an intersection, drove back the way I'd come. I parked the car in some heavy shadows, its grillwork pointed toward the city.

Getting out of the car, I crossed the street. At the mouth of the Cameron driveway, I stepped onto the grass. I took up a spot where shrubbery concealed me. I could watch the house and driveway. I could still get across the street, back to the car, quickly.

I began waiting.

The hardest part of it was to keep my mind from bounding around, overactive to make up for the inactivity of my body.

No one came out of the lighted house.

I felt the stirring of a night breeze off the bay. Through a hole in the shrubs, the lights on the mainland boulevard were visible. I watched the cars zipping along over there, little twinkling diamonds in the night.

The diamond chain began to stretch.

Finally it was a chain no longer, but individual winking lights that passed at varying intervals. The intervals got longer as night deepened.

The air had cooled a few degrees. Sweat, dried, gave my skin a stiff feeling.

I had been wrong.

It wouldn't happen tonight. Maybe tomorrow night or the next.

Or never. The whole guess might have been wrong from the beginning. In the light of everything that I'd dug out, the guess was right. But it was still nothing more than a reasonable assumption, and in Ivey's mind the assumption was reasonable that Nick Martin had killed the Yamashitas.

Suddenly my muscles went tight as a flare of light came from the house—light from the front door as it was opened.

I glimpsed Victor Cameron briefly as he came out of the house. He closed the door, and I turned and padded silently to the sidewalk.

I crossed the street and got in the borrowed buggy. I sat without turning on the motor or the lights.

The waiting this time was brief.

He was driving a Caddy, a cream-colored one with tail fins as big as a Buck Rogers rocket. I silently thanked him for owning a car like that, a standout that would be easy to follow.

The big car turned out of the driveway and nosed toward the city. It had taillights sufficient for a company of fire trucks.

I remained still until the taillights reached the distant intersection. They winked out, going to the left. Toward the mainland.

I let Cameron have a lead. He'd have to stop when he crossed the bridge, before he pulled onto the boulevard. There was only one direction for him to take, unless he turned around and stayed on the island a little longer. I was certain he wouldn't do that.

Mentally, I clocked the Caddy's progress. Then I started the borrowed car and went after him.

The twin banks of taillights made a right turn on the mainland boulevard as I crossed the short bridge.

Keeping Cameron in sight was no difficult trick. I knew the synchronization of the traffic lights. I shortened the gap when necessary to keep from catching a red light while he moved through green a block or two ahead.

I dropped farther back when he was out of the main business district. I drove past shanties, junk yards, welding shops.

He entered a narrow street where those inclined to escape the heat of rooms massed with sleeping bodies slept on rusty, iron-filigree balconies.

131

His destination was a gloomy apartment building on a dusty, brick-paved street on the edge of Ybor City.

The hulking building was four stories tall. The bottom level was occupied by a blaring juke joint, a pawn shop, and a palmist's establishment garish with signs proclaiming the wondrous powers of Madame Zecora, Gypsy Fortune-teller.

A wide doorway between the juke joint and pawn shop provided entrance to the apartment building.

Cameron stood for a short while when he got out of the Caddy. Then he crossed the street quickly and ducked inside the building.

I sat in the borrowed car and timed him. He was gone about five minutes. He went through a second hesitation as he came out of the building. There were few people outside. The only sign of life the block showed was the crowded gin mill.

His rapid steps returned Cameron to the Caddy. He sat there another ten minutes. Then, as if the strain were telling, he started the car and drove off with a roar of sudden power.

I got out of the car, knowing he hadn't found what he had come here to find. But he'd known where it was, and this was the place.

A fifteen-watt night light burned in the foyer of the building. A wide stairway, its treads scooped out by millions of shuffling footsteps, led upward. Beside the stairs, a narrow hall ran to the rear of the building. The building had the faint smell of sweat and of chitterlings cooked long ago.

At its birth, half a century or so ago, the building had possessed a certain elegance. There was a balustrade of heavy hardwood, scratched and scarred. The wainscoting was of marble. Stained and cracked, it had pieces missing, revealing the crumbling mortar cement underneath.

132

At the left was a row of mailboxes. Twelve apartments in the building, if the boxes were to be believed, four to each of the three upper floors.

One of the boxes was particularly dusty. She never got mail here, but the janitor, owner, or whoever looked after the building had dutifully scrawled her name on a slip of paper and stuck it to the box to match all the other boxes.

One greasy little slip of paper in all Tampa that stated simply: L. Shaw, 212.

CHAPTER **19** ▶▶▶ SOMEWHERE IN the upper reaches of the building a couple started fighting. A door slammed. The staccato of an angry man's footsteps came down the flights of stairs, a woman's bitter voice hurling invectives after him from the top floor.

I faded into the shadows beside the stairs. The man reached the foyer, thin as a blade in garish sport shirt and pegged pants. He dabbed at a scratch on his forehead below the line of black, curly hair. Cursing under his breath in Spanish, he vented his rage on the front door by kicking it open and disappearing outside.

Upstairs, the coarse voice of a male tenant told the raging dame to shut up. She told him where he could go. It seemed for a moment a cuss fight was starting, but the woman huffed into her apartment. The building quietened, letting the muffled beat of the juke box next door return to the walls like the pulse of a tired heart.

I slid from the shadows and padded up the stairs to the second floor. Number 212 fronted the street. The door was locked, and I took out my key ring. The old lock was not hard to pick.

I eased inside the apartment, closed and relocked the door. The air was stale and hot, a mingle of odors—the sweetish smell of powder and perfume overlaying the faint stench of old food and soured beer.

The old-fashioned roller blinds were half drawn, but enough light was admitted from the street for me to make out the shadows of furniture. With the pencil flash, I made a quick tour of the apartment.

It had been a dump to start with. She'd improved it none whatever. The lumpy living-room couch and chairs were littered with a few old newspapers and magazines. An ash tray had been spilled on the cracked linoleum, which was worn to the black asphalt base in spots. The kitchen was a mess, remains of old food on the table, dirty dishes piled in the sink, paper sacks holding empty beer cans and seeping garbage providing a popular rendezvous for the Florida variety of huge black roaches and swarming gnats.

There was a bed, dresser, and chest of drawers in the bedroom. The bed linens were soiled, mussed as if she had never made the bed. The dresser was dusty with spilled face powder, jumbled with an array of cosmetics. I glanced at the labels. She'd bought expensive beauty aids.

The closet was stuffed with clothing. All was in vulgar taste. The back corner of the closet was piled with soiled clothing.

I clicked off the flash, went to the kitchen, cracked a window.

I settled down inside for a wait, long or short.

About ten minutes later, a bell tinkled softly. Her telephone, which she'd had muffled. Twenty minutes after that, the discreet demand for her attention sounded again in the living room. I wondered if the caller were Cameron.

He'd expected to find her here tonight. I had the feeling she'd come.

The juke box in the gin mill kept up its whispered invasion of the walls. It became a normal part of the night, an unnoticed thing.

It was the sibilant background for the grating of a key in a lock.

I was on my feet, beside the door opening from the kitchen to the bedroom.

I heard her close the door. She stumbled against a piece of furniture and said, "Oh, damn!"

There were no wall switches here. She found the naked bulb hanging from its overhead wire. Light from the living room splashed into the bedroom. The silhouette of her came into the bedroom. She stretched, reaching for the socket holding the fly-specked bulb.

In the bedroom light, she sat down at the dresser and looked at herself a moment. The real she and the one in the mirror exchanged a soft, secretive little laugh.

She patted a yawn, lighted a cigarette, and reached for something on the floor at the end of the dresser.

She lifted into view an oval-shaped, deep hatbox that my rapid search with the pencil flash had missed.

She set the box on the dresser, but she didn't open it right away. She began working on her face, painting her lips as bright as fresh blood, touching the corners of her eyes with pencil, the lids with shadow. She made slight changes in the face, but the sum total of the change was great. The big change came from inside, as if the surface changes had wiped out the remaining curbs on her inner self.

The transformation from Rachie Cameron to Luisa Shaw was almost complete.

She opened the hatbox, lifted out the wooden form

holding the blonde headpiece. It was perfectly made and must have cost her quite a penny.

Pushing back her short-cut dark hair, she slipped the blonde headpiece on, working it carefully into place. It was the final detail needed to achieve the effect she was after.

She tilted her head, turned it from side to side, satisfying herself.

My throat clotted with something deeper than anger as I thought of the perverse pleasure and amusement she must have received the night we'd made the rounds together searching for a blonde woman in Ichiro Yamashita's life.

She let her fingertips caress the blonde hair, the headpiece that had shed a hair on the arm of Ichiro shortly before he died.

Dead and beautiful hair, like everything else about her.

I stepped inside the bedroom. Her upraised hand chilled in that position.

She was chilled all over for a moment. Then she turned to me slowly and said, "Hello, ugly man."

She rose gracefully, with that strength that comes from pliant, streamlined muscles.

"Have you waited long, ugly man?"

"Not enough to try my patience."

"I liked you," she said, coming toward me. "I thought about bringing you here."

"But you changed your mind."

"You were mean to me."

"That's too bad."

She slid her arms to my shoulders. "You went to a lot of trouble to find me."

"Considerable," I admitted. "It should have been easier. A long-dead blonde hair was found on Ichiro's arm. It must have been shed on him shortly before he died, or it would have got brushed off or fallen off. The lack of a dead per-

136

son to provide the hair indicated a wig. A wig indicated a masquerade, and a process of elimination indicated you as the person who'd delight in such a game. It wasn't clear at first. There were too many other details obscuring the picture."

"How much is clear now, ugly man?"

"Everything."

"Then you know I didn't kill anyone."

"You triggered five deaths by triggering the first, Ichiro's. You were the indirect, but major, cause behind a suffering, innocent man's going to jail."

"Oh, that. I'm not responsible for what other people do."

I gripped her wrists so hard she winced with pain. "You're very strong, ugly man," she said softly. "You're hurting me."

I looked at the avid sickness in her eyes and face, and shoved her away. "You're a sick little chick, Rachie. I wish there was some way to touch you once with real hurt. You deserve it."

Her lower lip dropped angrily. "I don't want any lectures! I don't want to hear about those stupid people!"

"Including the man unlucky enough to love you? Loving you, I guess, would be worse than being on heroin or taking poison. That's what you'd make it, Rachie. Torment, misery, poison."

"You shut up!"

"He went out there that afternoon, didn't he? To the Yamashita summerhouse. He found you and Ichiro together. . . ."

"You stinker! I don't have to listen—"

The breath went out of her as I cut off her attempt at flight by grabbing her, throwing her on the bed, and holding her with my knee in her midriff and my hands clutching her arms.

137

"And he couldn't stand it," I went on. "He grabbed up the nearest thing at hand, a metal lamp or book end or statuette. He clobbered Ichiro.

"I can imagine the quick way you played on his poisonous love for you. You got out of there. He was leaving, too, but the parents came home, into the house. They saw him. Now he was in the state of a jungle animal. It was kill or be killed for this man. He flattened Ichiro's father in the house, caught up with the fleeing little old lady on the front porch and let her have it there.

"Then, with every nerve screaming, every muscle crackling, every cell of him exploding, he thought of that other cottage, the Martins'. Had they seen? Must he silence them, too, in order to live? He ran there, found Nick asleep on the living-room couch. Perhaps he turned and started to go. Then it came to him. Here was safety. Here was a way out. There hung the samurai sword. Beside the couch was the whisky bottle. On the couch lay the sleeping man who sometimes went back in time when alcohol had blotted out his pain. Who went back and thought he had to kill Japanese again.

"So the man takes the sword and goes back to the Yamashita house and does what he thinks he has to do. He had not wanted to kill at all. Now he believed he was safe from the results of that blind, insane moment when he'd caught you and a man he'd believed a friend—"

"You'll pay for this," she gasped, her head rolling against the dirty linens. "I'll find a way—I'll make you pay."

"We'll collect a few other debts first," I said. "From the man. Remember him? The man who thought it was all over, until Sime Younkers stepped into the picture.

"If Sime had worked, instead of always looking for an easy buck, he'd have made a decent living. He had cunning. He had brains, twisted as they were. Delving into Ichiro's activities, Sime discovered your double life. As

138

efficient as a weasel, learning the truth about you since you were so much a part of Ichiro's activities, Sime sniffed possibilities, opportunities. Gleaning a knowledge of you and your acquaintances, he suspected the truth about what happened to the Yamashitas. For enough boodle, he would not only keep quiet, he would insure the murderer's safety for good by forcing Nick Martin into a jailhouse confession.

"Except, instead of paying Sime off with cash, the murderer made payment with something a lot more permanent.

"Safety was the thing our man wanted with all his tarnished soul. With Sime's death, he must have thought once again, the bloody path started in a wild moment of passion had ended.

"Then, all of a sudden, he was safe no longer. Tillie Rollo learned your whereabouts. You just couldn't stay away from it, could you? You contacted her. Tillie got the new phone number.

"At the outset, our man hadn't figured on me. But as time moved on, I got in his hair more and more. Suddenly I, if given the knowledge Tillie possessed, was very dangerous. He decided to set me up at Tillie's and get me off his neck once and for all. He was living from moment to moment, in desperation, trying to stamp out the fuses as his firecrackers got ready to explode.

"He got Tillie instead of me. It wasn't as good, for he knew now that as long as I lived, I'd be after him. But it gave him a chance for a breather, to try and think of something else."

Rachie-Luisa lay with the blonde hair framing her face. She was quiet now, staring at me.

"Do you know the man?"

"Yes. Prince Kuriacha."

"The big cluck fell like a ton of bricks for me."

"I'm sure you've enjoyed knowing that."

139

One of those lightning changes came into her eyes. "I really had him way out and gone. So much power over him."

"And through him over all of them. You deserve to die in a gutter, Rachie."

She breathed a laugh. "He told me that once himself. He had tears in his eyes. He said loving me was torture, but he couldn't do anything about it. He's been after me to go away with him."

"To a place of safety."

"That's right—but not without me."

Footsteps intruded into the muffled heartbeat of the walls. Footsteps on the bare flooring of the hallway.

They came to the door of 212.

They stopped. Someone knocked. Either her shattered father—or Kuriacha.

I eased away from Rachie.

"You make one move," I whispered, "and I'll make you wish he'd killed you."

CHAPTER **20** ▶ ▶ ▶ KURIACHA STOOD framed in the doorway, a dumb look on his heavy, swarthy face.

The love light left his muddy, yellow eyes as their ink-black centers looked down the muzzle of the .38.

"Come in, murderer," I invited, "and join our little group."

He didn't move until he saw my knuckle go white on the trigger. He edged into the room, moving lightly on his strong bandy legs. I toed the door closed.

He began to recover from his jolt. He turned his head

slowly on its thick, short column of neck and looked at
Rachie. Their eyes held a moment. Neither of them said
anything. The pulse beat of the gin mill undulated through
the walls.

"How'd he get here?" Kuriacha asked her in a ragged
whisper.

"He knows," Rachie said. "He knows it all now."

"How does he know?"

"Do you think I told him?"

"I don't know," he said. "I don't know what to think
any more."

"He figured it out for himself," Rachie said. "You
must have been real dumb in spots."

"He did pretty well," I said. "He had a long lead on
me to start with. He cut plenty of corners before I whittled
the lead down and jumped ahead of him. He's simple,
blunt, direct. So long as he stayed that way he was a
tough opponent. He made his slips when he paused and
started thinking."

Kuriacha's face was old and tired. "You wouldn't make
a deal? I've got a lot of money. I made as much money
in my time as some pretty fair movie stars."

"You're wasting your breath."

"I guessed I was. What put you onto me?"

"Several things, though I had to get the whole picture
before the details fell in place.

"When I ran into you in Ichiro's private apartment,
you were there to make sure nothing was around to con-
nect him with Luisa Shaw. You warned me off the case,
your only possible motive being to protect yourself and
Rachie, or Luisa, whichever you prefer to call her. You
tried to explain yourself by saying Sadao Yamashita's
brothers had been kind to you in your poverty-stricken
days in California. But he had no relatives out there, none
in this country at all. None to notify of his death, to take

141

care of the funeral arrangements. Victor Cameron had to attend to all those details himself. Sadao's relatives, except for his wife and son, were wiped out in Hiroshima.

"When I got out of the fire you lit in Sime Younkers' shack, you tried to trap me into revealing my location over the phone. Later, you tried to hunt me down in Ybor City. You were getting desperate. You had to nail me before I reached Rachie, through Tillie Rollo, and learned the whole truth. You made the final try at Tillie's place.

"You tailored the thing to fit yourself, Kuriacha, down to having the stomach to mutilate the Yamashitas and kill twice again to protect yourself.

"Now you're a dead duck, buster. I've got a slug—the one that killed Tillie—that I'm sure will match a gun belonging to you. I'll have a blonde wig, plus Victor Cameron. When he knows the truth can't be hidden any longer, he'll talk. It won't matter to him.

"Given a picture he can't deny or ignore, Steve Ivey will wrap up the details. His lab boys will come up with bits of proof you don't even suspect exist."

Kuriacha stood with his arms dangling like those of a great ape. Sweat gathered in heavy drops and ran down the sides of his face.

"He's failed to add one thing, Prince," Rachie said softly. "What he says is true, but he's the only one so far who knows. This is your last chance. They'll put you in the electric chair."

"Rivers has the gun," I reminded them.

"You nearly broke Rivers in little pieces once," she told him.

"That was the prelim," I said. "This is the rubber match, the one that counts."

"That's right, Prince, this is the big one," Rachie said.

He knuckled a drop of sweat from the end of his thick, flat nose. He looked at the gun.

142

"Don't be a fool," I said. "Don't let her talk you into the final mistake."

"I don't have to talk him into anything," she said, turning toward me. "He doesn't have any choice left."

She'd lifted her hand to the side of her face. With a quick motion, she tore the wig off, slapped me hard across the eyes, and said, "Now!"

The blonde strands slashed my eyes stingingly. All his years of training went into the movement of the great ape.

I pulled the trigger and knew I'd missed. I tried to rock back, swing the gun around.

He hit me like a two-hundred-pound sack of bricks shot out of the end of a gun. We splintered a rickety end table and the wall slammed against my back.

His face had darkened, the lips and eyes pulled tight. He grabbed for my throat with one hand and reached for the gun with the other. My gun hand stayed out of his way for a second. To do so, it had to bear away from his.

I hit him twice in the side of the face with my free hand. He didn't bother to shake off the punches. He simply took them, and kept trying for the gun.

He'd failed to grab my throat. Instead, he'd got his palm under my chin and was trying to grind the back of my head through the wall.

He took a chance by slipping the palm free and going after the gun with both hands.

He locked his fingers on my wrist. He was off balance with the effort. I peeled off the wall and we swung to the middle of the room. His feet tangled in the wreckage of the end table.

I added the final pressure and he went down, twisting the gun.

The gun went off. The bullet hit him in the chest. It knocked a gasp from him, and his eyes went wide. He

143

reared up and the gun squirted out of my fingers and skidded across the grimy floor.

Kuriacha fell back and I pulled free of him. I grabbed the arm of a chair to help get my feet under me.

"That's far enough, Ed," Rachie said. She stood near the doorway, holding the gun.

I took a weaving step toward her. Her eyes glinted. "I wouldn't be afraid. Not the least bit afraid."

Kuriacha pulled himself around on the floor, his strength spent, and reached an imploring hand toward her. "Luisa . . ."

Without bothering to look at him, she backed through the door, closed it.

Kuriacha lay holding the red spot on his chest.

"She's gone."

"It looks that way," I said.

His breathing was loud and hard in the dead heat of the room.

"She won't come back."

"Not if she can help it."

His eyes were glazed with pain. "I don't understand it, Rivers."

"That's tough."

"I loved her."

"That's even tougher."

"Where will she go? What will she do?"

"Find another Kuriacha, if she makes it out of Tampa."

"And never remember . . . I should have killed her in the beginning, instead of the others."

"You should never have killed anyone."

"I didn't want to. But after Ichiro . . ." Raw fear blotted out the pain glaze, fear of the picture that he suddenly had of himself. "What happened to me, Rivers?"

"I guess the head shrinkers could think of plenty of theories," I said. "For my money, you had it in you all the time, the callousness, the brutality, the selfish viciousness. You drank her in like an alcoholic crazy for booze, with no thought of control. You had to kill a part of yourself before you could kill any of the others, because it was in the way of the debased part. It was your choice. So, in short, you're an s.o.b. who deserves the electric chair."

I turned to the phone, picked it up, dialed. While I waited for headquarters to answer, I noticed a new quality in the room.

The insidious pulse beat had gone out of the walls.

CHAPTER **21** ▶ ▶ ▶ SIX MONTHS LATER, I noticed two items in a newspaper that cleared up the tag ends of the Yamashita case.

I was sitting in a quiet, clean, sunny room as I looked through the paper. My mind wasn't much on the news until I saw the first of those two items.

It was date-lined Atlanta. It concerned the death of a "hostess" at an oft-raided Atlanta clip joint. The coroner had rendered a verdict of accidental death. The inquest had shown that she'd boozed herself to the teeth with bootleg whisky. It had poisoned her. She had been identified as Rachie Cameron, daughter of a former Tampa businessman.

The second item was headed VETERAN'S HOSPITAL SURGEONS SAY NEW SPINE SURGERY TECHNIQUE WILL SUPPLANT ALL OTHERS.

I lowered the paper and looked across the hospital waiting room at Helen Martin.

145

Her steady eyes met mine. She managed a smile. "They're almost through in surgery, Ed."

"We'll know in a little while."

One thing I knew already. The country Nick had fought for had never stopped trying.

That kind of persistence can be defeated again and again.

But not for keeps.

Printed in the United States
By Bookmasters